# HERE'S TO YOU, ZEB PIKE

## JOHANNA PARKHURST

Harmony Ink

Published by
Harmony Ink Press
5032 Capital Circle SW
Suite 2, PMB# 279
Tallahassee, FL 32305-7886
USA
publisher@harmonyinkpress.com
http://harmonyinkpress.com

Here's to You, Zeb Pike
© 2013 Johanna Parkhurst.

Cover Art
© 2013 Anne Cain.
annecain.art@gmail.com
Cover content is for illustrative purposes only and any person depicted on the cover is a model.

ISBN: 978-1-62798-524-6
Library ISBN: 978-1-62798-526-0
Digital ISBN: 978-1-62798-525-3


Printed in the United States of America
First Edition
November 2013

Library Edition
February 2014

For Mom, Dad, and Anthony. For everything.

# ACKNOWLEDGMENTS

THIS BOOK exists because of a lot of people.

This book exists because of the students in four different middle schools in four different cities. Thanks, guys, for constantly inspiring me, keeping me on all ten of my toes, and never letting me forget why I write.

This book exists because of the amazing friends and family members who read draft after draft and kept telling me not to give up on it.

And this book definitely only exists because of Travis, my lifelong cheerleader and editor. There's no one I would rather explore life's paths with.

# PROLOGUE

SOMETIMES I wonder if I'm the only high school freshman on the planet who actually likes school.

Well, I guess I don't really like school itself. I don't really enjoy writing papers or listening to lectures or dealing with quadratic formulas or any of that stuff. It would probably be more accurate to say that I like *resting*.

School is one of the few places where I get a chance to relax, sit back, and not think too hard. My buddy Race hates when I talk like that—he says it's egotistical of me to brag that I can ignore about 80 percent of what our teachers say and still get the grades I do—but I'm not trying to brag. That's just how school is for me.

Take the class I'm currently chilling out in: history with Ms. Carlson. This is a class that probably makes other freshmen want to slit their throats. I mean, I know all students think their teachers drone on and on, but Ms. Carlson brings it to the level of an art form. She must have been absent from teacher school on the day "class discussion" was introduced as a method of instruction.

Me? I love this class. Most of the time I completely zone out for forty minutes and just recap whatever I missed with a little textbook skimming during study hall.

Today I've managed to lean back my chair as far as it will go, and I've got my feet propped up on my backpack. I'm half-listening to Ms. Carlson; she's going on about the Pike Expedition. After all, this is Colorado Springs, home of Pikes Peak, the semifamous and epically huge mountain that is currently looming right outside our classroom window.

"Zebulon Pike and his team did attempt to ascend the peak, but they were forced to turn back, essentially due to weather conditions and a lack of appropriate gear. There were no REIs in the area then, you see."

The class titters, which is more of an effort to keep Ms. Carlson smiling than a nod to how great the joke is. Ms. Carlson is one of those teachers who enjoys thinking she's hilarious. We're a bunch of students who enjoy inflated grades.

"Wait, Ms. Carlson, I don't get it. Do you mean he didn't get to the top?"

Ms. Carlson looks annoyed by the interruption, and I'm pretty sure it's not just because Albert Lansing forgot to raise his hand. I'm telling you, this is not a woman who appreciates student involvement in her classes.

"No, Albert, he did not. Now, shortly after the Pike team was forced to abandon the—"

"Wait, wait, wait." Now Dani Gonzalez is interrupting Ms. Carlson's thoughts, also without raising her hand. Definitely not good for Ms. Carlson's composure. "Why is the mountain named after him? Why is it named Pikes Peak if Zebulon Pike didn't climb it?"

Ms. Carlson takes a moment to collect herself before she addresses Dani. Her lips are pursed so tight they could easily disappear. That would probably make speaking difficult, which would make her teaching nonexistent.

"The mountain is named Pikes Peak because Zebulon was the one who first *discovered* it, Danielle. Whether or not he reached the top of it is hardly the point."

James Fuerte raises his hand, and Ms. Carlson calls on him. It's a foregone conclusion that she doesn't want to, but at this point her flow has to be shot anyway. "But there were already Native

American tribes that had been living in this area for hundreds of years; wouldn't it be more accurate to say *they* discovered the mountain? Shouldn't it be named after them?"

James is smart. He knows Ms. Carlson loves to talk about how the land we live on was stolen from the Native Americans. She'll have to get sucked into this now.

"You are correct, Mr. Fuerte. The mountain had been *discovered* long before Zebulon arrived. It would be much more accurate for us to say that Zebulon first recorded the existence of the mountain." She shakes her head at the flurry of hands that go up in the air. "That said, the fact that he did not climb the mountain himself is entirely irrelevant. History has shown us time and again that discoveries are far more important than conquests."

I'm actually paying attention for once, and I sort of would like her to expand on that point, but she goes off into how Zebulon Pike's team was captured by the Spanish.

While Ms. Carlson heads with Zeb Pike's team and the Spanish authorities to Santa Fe, I stay comfortably at the side of Pikes Peak, wondering if Ms. Carlson is right. I just can't see it. My life proves over and over again that discoveries don't matter at all; you have to conquer what life throws at you if you want to get anywhere in this world.

The fact that my brother and sister and I aren't in foster care is proof enough of that. I "discovered" early on in our lives that my parents were basically worthless, as parents go. That discovery? All it meant was that I had to conquer taking care of Matt and Julia at, like, age ten.

The results of that conquest, I'm proud to say, have so far been pretty positive. Take today: it's one of those sunny, balmy days that can still appear in September in Colorado. I've promised to take Matt and Julia to the park this afternoon, and we're going to have a great time. My friend Race is coming too, which means I'll get to use his skateboard a few times, and Matt is hilarious in the park. He's a great soccer player, and he loves to show off his skills. He used to play for one of the city teams when he was younger, but we haven't had that kind of money in a few years.

And all that great family bonding will be brought to us because *I* conquered learning how to do laundry and make dinner before social services could figure out that my mother can't find our apartment most nights. I don't think discovering the laundry was sitting by the hamper really got me anything.

Ms. Carlson is still going on about Zebulon Pike and the Spanish, and I go back to relaxing.

I run a quick mental check to see if there's anything I should be worrying about right now. Life seems to be treating me better than it treated Zeb Pike during the Pike Expedition, because I can't come up with anything. The money Mom left us a week or so ago is stretching. We're eating a lot of ramen and frozen dinners, but Matt and Julia like that kind of stuff, so they don't seem to care. The electricity is still on. I don't know if the gas still is, but we can worry about that when it really starts to get cold. I'm pretty sure Mom paid the rent through the end of the month. Things are working out a lot better than the last time Mom took off—that time she'd forgotten to pay the electric bill, and I had to track down Dad and get money from him to pay it.

Things seem to be going okay. I mean, at least I'm not stuck in waist-deep snow on the side of a mountain and about to accidentally stumble directly into Spanish territory.

The school secretary, Mrs. McMann, comes to the door and motions for Ms. Carlson. Ms. Carlson puts off her lecture long enough to walk to the door and read the note Mrs. McMann passes her. "Dusty," she calls out. "The front office needs you."

I pull myself up out of my cramped desk chair to go see Mrs. McMann, the tiniest secretary in the history of school secretaries. I like the woman and all, but she truly is miniscule. She can't be more than five feet tall. I'm only in the ninth grade, and I tower over her.

McMann is frowning intently at me. "Dusty, I need you to downstairs with me for a bit. Julia seems to be pretty sick, and n't get your mother on the phone. She's not answering her ber. I called the work number she listed, but the person who ed said she no longer works there."

4

Of course they had…. Mom hasn't been at that temp job in nearly six months. My mom takes the phrase "temporary" to a whole new level. I reflect briefly on how impressive it is that the school hasn't needed to reach Mom in that long, and I have a moment of pride. Who needs parents, anyway? We're doing just fine.

I pause my inner monologue of what an amazing brother I am to notice that Mrs. McMann is nervously tapping her foot, which instantly makes *me* nervous. Mrs. McMann has been Prescott Charter School's secretary for a long time, and she knows the difference between a sick kid and a faking one. She also knows Matt and Julia pretty well, so Julia must be in bad shape if Mrs. McMann thinks I need to be pulled out of class.

I practically race down the stairs to the health room, all the while worrying myself into a panic. Julia hardly ever gets sick—she hasn't even had a cold for the past few months. I start to wonder if a person can get sick from eating too much ramen. By the time I reach poor Jules, I've completely remade our grocery list in my head and added about twelve green vegetables to it.

The health room reeks of vomit. Julia's lying on her side on an old green cot, her skin as white as the ugly fluorescent light in our apartment hallway. Her light-blond hair is stuck to her face with sweat, and she's holding her stomach. "Dusty," she whispers, "I threw up twice."

"Aw, that's okay." I sigh. "Just lie there for a second." I sit down next to her and put her head in my lap. Her forehead feels like someone could cook an egg on it.

I look up at Mrs. McMann. "Can I please take her home? Please? She looks horrible."

Mrs. McMann hesitates. "Maybe we should try your mother's cell again. We really need to get her to come take Julia. I can't release her to you like that. Anyway, how would you get her home? She's in no shape to walk."

I suck in a breath and release it slowly. This is definitely a challenge. How am I going to get Julia home without anyone realizing that our mother is MIA? "Mom just got a new job with the temp agency, and I don't know her office number. She won't be home until at least five. Please let me take her, Mrs. McMann. I'll take good care of her; you know I will. She can piggyback home with me. She's too sick to stay here." I give Mrs. McMann my best puppy-dog face and hope I look like the upstanding, perfect student I always try so hard to be at Prescott Charter School. I know I have a pretty good shot of her saying yes. Prescott doesn't have a school nurse full-time, and if Julia stays here, Mrs. McMann will have to take care of her.

She hesitates for a moment, and I feel suddenly powerful. If I get away with this lie, I can get away with anything when it comes to my brother and sister. I am really in charge of their lives, even if no one else knows it.

I wonder what my parents would think of that.

"You're sure there isn't another number I can call?"

I shake my head. Odds are Mom doesn't even have that cell phone Mrs. McMann's been calling all morning. My mother changes cell phones almost weekly, depending on which pay-as-you-go company she's using that week, and she never bothers to leave me a new number.

"Let me check with Mrs. Sabring," Mrs. McMann finally decides. Mrs. Sabring is Prescott's principal. She's known my family for a very long time, since I was in first grade, and if anyone is going to blow my cover, it will be her.

Mrs. Sabring comes in and looks Julia over. Jules whimpers and clings to my hand. "And you don't know your mother's new work number, Dusty?" Mrs. Sabring asks, her face etched with concern.

I shake my head. "Un-uh. And she never gets home till late."

"Well… I suppose I can let you take her. On two conditions: I will drive you both home, and you are to have your mother call me immediately when she gets home tonight."

"Of course, Mrs. Sabring." I agree with that same upstanding nod, even though I have no idea how "Mom" is going to call that night. At this point, I don't care much. All I want to do is get Julia home and in bed.

I stop by Mrs. Hall's algebra class to ask Race to pick up Matt, and bring him home. Race keeps my secrets well. He's the kind of friend you can make farting noises with during lunch and still trust to never tell anyone that you almost set his mother's couch on fire in the fourth grade. I'm never sure which quality I appreciate more.

I help Julia into Mrs. Sabring's car. She whines and groans, and for a minute I'm afraid she's going to throw up all over the expensive-looking interior of Mrs. Sabring's sedan. "Probably just that nasty flu bug going around," Mrs. Sabring says as she drives us down the street to our apartment complex. "Everybody's coming down with it. Make sure you give her lots of fluids, Dusty."

At home Julia shows no signs of improvement. I follow all Mrs. Sabring's flu instructions, but none of it seems to help. Jules throws up every glass of water I give her. She whimpers more loudly each hour, holding her stomach more firmly every time she grabs it. I try to take her temperature on our old, beat-up thermometer, but it says she has a fever of 110 degrees. I know that can't be right, but she definitely has a fever. Her forehead feels like a fire pit.

By the time Matt and Race get to the apartment around three-thirty, I'm starting to freak out. Matt comes racing up the hallway and into the doorway shouting, "Dusty! Is Julia okay, is she okay?"

I stop him at the door to Julia's bedroom. "Shut up, kiddo," I whisper, bumping my shoulder into his to let him know I'm not mad. "She's finally sleeping." And she is, a little. She's dozing on and off, but she wakes up periodically to tell me how much her stomach hurts and throw up again. Nothing stays down.

Matt nods and tiptoes into Julia's room. He sits down on the bed with her and frowns hard, as if he's trying to diagnose her just by looking at her. Matt's a really funny kid. Most of the time he's a bundle of energy, loose and fun, like a lot of other eight-year-olds I've met. But there are some things he takes very seriously. His teacher has told me that Matt will be a class clown all day long, but when it comes time for math, which is the subject Matt enjoys the most and is best at, he settles right down and becomes the helper for his entire group. Matt takes Julia very seriously too. He hardly ever fights with her, even though they are really close in age and Julia can be pretty whiny sometimes. He seems to have endless patience when it comes to her. Julia was really young when Mom and Dad started skipping out on us, and Matt always seems very aware of that.

Six-year-old Julia's not the laid-back kid Matt is—she's much more deliberate and careful. She picks out her clothes carefully (even though we never have the money to buy her anything all that great), she fixes her hair carefully, she eats carefully. When she does her homework, she takes almost an hour to write a paragraph—not because she's slow, but because every letter she puts on the paper has to be perfectly formed. It cracks me up, except when we're in a hurry and she's taking two hours to pick out the perfect pink outfit.

I wish she could be sitting at the kitchen table right now, taking twenty minutes to write her name at the top of her paper, instead of lying in her bed looking like she's never going to stand up again.

Race pulls me backward out of the room a little ways. "Dude, is she okay? She doesn't look so great."

I run my hand over my forehead. "Race, I don't know what to do. Her fever's really high and she won't stop throwing up."

Race looks in on Matt and Julia. He shakes his head slowly, tongue between his teeth. This is Race's "thinking" look. Normally I'd make some joke about how much brain power he's wasting just keeping his tongue in place, but I don't have the energy right now.

"Man...." Race pauses. "I'm not sure you have any more choices, Dusty."

Even before he says it, I know he's right.

WE CAN both see that Julia is in no position to be carried anywhere, so Race decides to call his mom and see if she'll bring us to the clinic near our house. We agree to try to hold up the pretense that

8

my mom is at work for as long as possible, even though I don't think it will hold up very long if anything is really wrong with Jules. Still, it's worth a shot.

I unsuccessfully take Julia's temperature one more time and try not to wince every time she moans while Race is on his cell phone. "Yeah, Ma, Dusty's sister is really sick, and his parents are at work. No, we can't reach them. Could you give them a ride to the clinic? Yeah, thanks, Mom." He hangs up. "She'll be here in twenty minutes."

At some point I start to think this might be the longest twenty minutes of my life. Julia's whimpers are getting more and more pronounced, and Matt finally turns away from her a little. Race is sitting on the floor, staring at the ceiling. It's horrible.

At least Race's mom, Barbara, is great. She really likes Matt and Julia anyway, and she keeps Matt distracted in the front seat of the car while Race and I hold Julia in the back. At the clinic, she fills out all the paperwork for us so I won't have to stop holding Julia at all. She does look concerned, though, and I don't like that very much.

Julia's still on my lap, and I'm glancing at the stupid signs around me—"Wash your hands to wash away worries"—when I notice the insurance information paper Barbara is filling out. I feel a spear of panic jab into my spine. I don't even know what health care plan Julia has—I know it's the state one, but I don't know anything else about it, and I don't have that much money from the stash Mom left. Are they going to refuse to see Julia?

Barbara is next to me, asking me questions about Jules as she fills out the clinic paperwork. "Uh, Barbara?" I mumble. "I think I have a problem. I don't have any money with me."

Barbara doesn't take her eyes off the paperwork. "Don't worry about it, Dusty. I'll help you." Maybe she sees a look cross my face, because she pats my knee and says, "I'll talk to your mom about all this later."

Her mouth gets tight when she says that. She's never said anything to me, but I'm pretty sure Barbara doesn't think too much of my mom. That's fine with me—I don't think too much of her either most of the time.

"Julia Porter," a nurse calls from the hallway.

I hold Jules, who is sleepy and dazed, against me, and Race and I half-carry her into the room. I help her lie down on the padded exam table, where she curls up and starts sucking her thumb. Normally I hate when Julia sucks her thumb (she is six years old—it seems babyish to me), but this time I don't try to stop her.

Race leaves the room to wait with his mom, and I stand there, my arms crossed tightly across my chest and my hands balled up into fists. The doctor is taking forever. Every time Julia cries, I want to run into the hallway and grab the first person I see in scrubs.

Finally the doctor comes in. He pokes and prods Julia and asks her all kinds of weird questions before he announces what I hear as my own death sentence: "You need to get her to a hospital immediately. Her appendix is close to bursting."

Julia's whimper is about the only thing that stops me from putting my fist through the wall. Julia will be okay once we got to the hospital, but this is the end of my family. The doctors there will notice that neither of our parents ever show up, and Matt and Julia will be taken away from me. I'll never see them again.

The doctor must notice how shaky I suddenly look. "Now, it's nothing to be that concerned about. It will require an operation, but you caught it in time. She'll be just fine, I promise."

*Easy for you to say, doc.*

I have a momentary flashback to Ms. Carlson's lecture *du jour*. This must be what Zeb felt like when he realized the snow was only getting deeper… and the mountain was only getting higher.

# CHAPTER ONE

*SEVEN YEARS Earlier*

*"Dusty, can you change Matt's diaper?"*

*Dusty stared at his mother. She was on the phone, cigarette smoke hanging around her head like a fading halo, cackling and laughing over the sound of the crying baby in the next room.*

*Dusty hated changing his brother's diaper, but he also didn't want to listen to Matt scream anymore, so he put down the Transformer he'd been playing with and headed into the bedroom he shared with the baby.*

*Matt's face was so red Dusty wondered if he might explode. Dusty found a clean diaper in a box next to the crib and started unsnapping Matt's dirty onesie. It looked like his mother had forgotten to do the laundry again.*

*Matt finally calmed down and put his fist into his mouth. He studied Dusty as he chewed on his hand, and Dusty couldn't help but smile. Matt almost always stopped crying when Dusty held him, which was something their mother certainly couldn't say.*

*Now that Matt was quiet, Dusty could hear his mother's loud voice traveling from the next room.*

*"Donna, I just can't handle it sometimes! I swear, that man is driving me crazy... yes, he lost another paycheck. Poker, this time, I think. Well, he was drunk, of course.*

11

*"What do you mean, how do I let it happen? You've met Luke. You know how he can be. He said the incident at Lucky Dames was the last time he was going to let that happen...*

*"Oh God, I'd love to go with you. I can't wait until Dusty's old enough to take care of Matt all night so I can finally get away from here for longer than a few hours."*

She started whispering then, which always made Dusty nervous. What was she talking about now? He finished getting the new diaper on his brother and latched it as tightly as he could. The sounds from the next room suggested his Mom was finally off the phone and maybe even making dinner.

*"Abby!"*

The sounds of his father coming home filled the apartment. Dusty moved toward the doorway to say hello before he decided to wait a few minutes. It was usually better to see what kind of mood Dad was in before talking to him. He'd know it was a good mood if his father was laughing and calling his mother *"Abbero;"* growling and yelling meant a bad mood that Dusty would hide out in his room to avoid.

*"Woman, I keep telling you not to worry about that! I got more money coming in, I swear."*

Uh-oh. A bad mood. Dusty lifted Matt out of his crib so he could play on the dingy apartment carpet. It was looking like they were going to be in here for a while.

His father's yelling became so loud that Dusty was pretty sure the neighbors could hear. *"Pregnant? What you do mean you might be pregnant again? You don't need no stinkin' test! We just had another kid."*

More yelling and some crying, but Dusty couldn't make out words anymore. He was pretty sure it was his mom who was crying.

*"Geez, I can't even listen to you when you get like this! I gotta get out of here."* Then the door slammed again, and soon all Dusty could hear was his mother sobbing in the next room.

Matt giggled and held his arms out to be picked up. Dusty lifted him in the air and tried to pretend it was just the two of them in the apartment.

ON THE way to the hospital, Race's mom chats with Matt in the front seat while Race and I conspire in the back. "Maybe you can tell them your Mom works nights," he whispers.

"Stupid, Julia will be in the hospital for days."

"Should we tell my Mom? Maybe she can help us," Race whispers back.

"No way," I answer quickly. That will blow everything.

I'm being taken down by a bodily organ that doesn't even have a purpose—except, apparently, to destroy Dusty Porter's life.

The hospital gets Julia into surgery quickly—the clinic must have called ahead. Then Race, Barbara, Matt and I are left alone in the waiting room, and I decide it is probably time to do something. Barbara keeps asking me if I've gotten in touch with our parents yet, and my whole "waiting for them to get home" story is starting to sound shady even to me.

Producing my parents isn't all that easy. If it was, I probably wouldn't have had to figure out what fabric softener is three years ago. Dad hasn't lived with us in years, but at least he still lives in Colorado Springs, and I can usually find him if I really need him. Who knows where Mom is? When she disappears, she *disappears.* She once came home with a story of some friend who took her to Florida.

It seems like locating Dad is my best option.

I ask Race if he wants to find a vending machine with me to get Matt some soda. We're barely at the machine before I drop my plan on him.

"Look, I gotta go find my dad. Can you cover for me for a few hours?"

Race nearly chokes on the piece of gum he has in his mouth. "Are you crazy? A few hours? Where am I supposed to tell them you went for a few hours?"

I run my hands through my hair, hoping the plan I've been forming in my head isn't going to sound incredibly stupid coming out of my mouth. "I'll tell your mom that my mom still isn't answering her phone. Then I'll say I need to go back home and tell her what's going on. Then I'll just come back with Dad instead. No big deal. It'll take me awhile to come back… just keep telling her that I must've had to wait for Mom or something."

Race pinches his eyebrows together. "I dunno, Dusty… you really wanna do this?"

Is he crazy? "What else do you expect me to do? I have like ten minutes until your mother realizes something is up and starts questioning me hardcore."

Race rubs the tip of his blue Converse sneaker into the vomit-colored hospital linoleum below him. "Maybe… tell her what's going on?"

I stare at him, wondering if I've ever actually met this guy before. Maybe he has appendicitis too…. He must have a fever to be talking like this. "Are you serious?"

He stubs his toe a little harder into the linoleum and keeps his eyes on the floor. "Yeah. I mean, you can't keep this up forever, Dusty. You've always known that."

"What's that supposed to mean?" I snarl, forcing him to look up at me. "I've done this for a long time, Race, and I can keep doing it. All I need is *someone to cover for me.*" I put as much emphasis on those last few words as possible.

I've known Race since the third grade, when we discovered we shared a common passion for Pokemon. We gave up on Pokemon a long time ago, but Race has stayed the one guy in the world I can trust. He's cool to hang out with and yet still very rational and loyal—an awesome friend. It almost feels like the image I have of him in my head is fading, and it's being replaced by a blurry, confused vision of the kid I've known since I was eight. Race looks around the room for a few minutes before he glances at me again.

"Fine, dude. I'll cover for you." I turn to walk out and he grabs the shoulder of my jacket. "Just… be careful, okay? And don't take too long."

"Sure. And hey, could you do me a favor? Make sure Matt and Jules know I'm coming back, okay?"

Race only looks puzzled by that for a second before it seems to connect in his head and he nods. "Course, dude." I can see worry lines adding up across his forehead. "Where do you think your dad is this time, anyway?"

I shrug. "I'll start with that apartment complex he was living in a few months ago. Who cares? I'll find him. Just make sure you cover for me, okay? Especially to your mom, and to the school if anybody calls from there." I don't know if Barbara has gotten in touch with them.

"Sure. Man, it's a good thing you guys all go to the same school."

He's right. There aren't a lot of K-12 schools in the city, and Prescott Charter School is one of the few. If I had to go to a regular high school when I started my freshman year this fall, someone in administration would have noticed pretty quickly what was going on with our family. But Prescott is small enough for me to watch the kids and make sure things don't look too sketchy with our parents. I'm always there to come up with some answer for why Mom and Dad can't make it to a meeting or a field trip.

"You're not gonna try to track down your mom?" Race asks, stubbing the heel of his wide sneaker into the linoleum this time.

"Nah. You know how hard she is to find. She's probably not even in the Springs. At least Dad's always around here somewhere."

"You got any money?"

"What do you think?" I snap.

Race reaches into his sock and pulls out a ten, which he slaps into my hand. "Bus fare. No sweat. Take it, okay?"

I raise an eyebrow at him. "I bet there's tons of sweat all over this."

Race whacks me in the stomach. "Ya, beats whatever your socks smell like right now."

I look down at the money in my hand, wishing I could hand it back and say I don't need it. Race is always way too generous with

15

his money. Once he bought Julia this brand-new Barbie she wanted because he knew I could never afford it. I hold that thought in my head for a moment before I curl the bill up into my pocket. I've got a limited amount of time to find my dad, and trying to do the whole thing on foot or hitchhiking isn't going to help.

I grin at Race. "Thanks, Track." I enjoy coming up with new ways of torturing him about his name. It's his mom's maiden name or something. It would be a complete liability to anyone else, but not Race. Somehow it works for him.

"Whatever, Dirt pile." His nickname for me isn't all that clever, but creativity is not Race's strong suit.

"Look...," I add as we walk toward the waiting room, "whatever happens... make sure the kids know I haven't left them. That's the most important thing."

"Yeah.... I know."

The picture of Race clears in my head again.

I look over at Matt, who is totally engrossed in a cartoon he's watching with some other kids in the waiting room. That's the most important thing.


"WHAT DO you mean you have to go wait for your mom at home? You still can't reach her?"

Barbara isn't swallowing my story as quickly and easily as I hoped she would. This is going to be harder than I thought.

"There's no answer at her work, and she still isn't answering her cell. And we don't have a phone at home." That's true. It's been shut off for months now.

Barbara rubs her face in exasperation. "Fine. Let's go. I'll drive you to the apartment."

"You can't!" Even I know my voice gets too sharp then, as Barbara looks up in confusion and Race gives me a warning glance. "Uh... someone has to wait here in case Julia wakes up or something."

"Okay. You and Race stay here and I will go to your apartment to wait for your mom."

Hmm. This is definitely going to be harder than I thought.

"Umm… no. That won't work either."

"Why not?" Barbara sighs.

"It's just… my mom doesn't know you all that well. She's not gonna want to find you in her house telling her that her daughter has appendicitis."

Barbara sighs. "Dusty, let me understand this. You want me to send you home—alone at night, and without a ride—to tell your mom where your sister is, while Race and I wait here with Matt?"

"Yes." I try to pull out that same "upstanding" look I used earlier on Mrs. Sabring. "You don't have to worry about me, Barbara. I know how to take the bus. And actually, it's only like five thirty. It won't really be dark for another hour."

I'm actually a little surprised when she agrees.

I head for the hospital lobby, feeling apprehensive. I'm pretty sure I'll be able to find my dad, and I'm also pretty sure he'll come back to the hospital with me once he knows how sick Julia is. But I can't shake the gut feeling it might not be that easy. It sure wouldn't be the first time my unpredictable and freewheeling father didn't say what I wanted to hear from him.

I FIND my way to the bus stop outside the hospital and wait, staring down the Front Range mountains in front of me.

The Front Range is pretty impressive, even if you've been looking at it your whole life. It's a span of enormous mountains, rocky and tree-covered, almost purple-colored. And yes, these are the "purple mountain majesties" from the song "America the Beautiful." (Believe me when I say every kid who's ever spent more than five minutes in a Colorado Springs elementary school can recite that song backward and forward.) Right in the center of them

17

is good old Pikes Peak: fourteen thousand feet of mountain that, apparently, its own namesake couldn't even climb.

Who would think that right now I'd find Colorado History class to be a helpful distraction?

The thing is, I've grown up in Colorado Springs, and these mountains are part of my life, part of my existence. They've always been a constant in my life, and I appreciate that about them. Except for the coats of snow that sometimes cover them, they never change.

They are the one and only thing, I sometimes think, that never change. I'm still staring at them as the bus arrives.

When I last saw my dad, he was living in the Lakeview Apartment complex on Circle Drive. The name's about as deceiving as it gets. The only water anywhere nearby is this tiny pond in the courtyard of the apartments. I figure the name needs to be deceiving because the apartments are so disgusting. All four buildings in the complex have peeling brown paint, carpet that is probably older than me, and month-to-month renters who've got to cheer the day they finally save up enough to move down the road to an apartment with an actual view of something besides brown grass. The upper central area of Colorado Springs, where the apartments are, is not exactly known for its quality living. The southwest area is really high-class, and the north end too. But the upper central part of the city tends to be known for its low-income housing and bars.

We live in the lower center of town, which isn't much better than what's directly above it, but that doesn't make it any easier to go visit my dad. The last time I stopped by (it was less stopping by and more begging for grocery money), his place was packed with unemployed guys who apparently had nothing better to do than sit around a dirty apartment all day.

My dad swears he makes pretty good money, but that always seems sketchy to me. I have a good idea what he does for that money.

It doesn't help that I always feel like I'm getting ready to do battle when I go looking for Dad, which I sort of am. He always gets angry with me for letting Mom disappear, even though there's never anything I can do about that. Then he goes off about how she must've left us with plenty of money; how could we have run out so quickly?

He hasn't lived with us in so long anyway that most of the time it's easier just to pretend he doesn't exist. He only comes by the apartment to see Matt and Julia once every couple of months. I swear that if I didn't need the money, I'd have stopped going to see him years ago.

I get to Circle okay, and I stand in front of his apartment complex for a second before I get up the nerve to go into the unlocked front door and up the stairs to the apartment. I stare at the bell as if I can will it to ring itself, but I quickly remember I don't have time to goof around and press the white button.

I can hear whooping and laughing, surrounded by loud music, coming through the door. Just Dad's environment.

The guy who answers the door is skinny and balding, about thirty, with really bad teeth. I recognize him as my Dad's friend Seth, but he sure doesn't recognize me. "Who the heck are you?" he practically snarls, lighting a cigarette as he speaks. I clear my throat to be heard over the music and try to stand up to my full five feet seven inches. It's moments like these I wish I was taller; maybe that would make me look like someone this guy would listen to.

"I'm looking for Luke. I'm his son."

Seth chokes on the some of the smoke drifting up around his face. "Luke's got a kid?"

Seth has met me a bunch of times, and Matt and Julia too, actually, but I decide not to bring that up just then. "Yeah. Three of us. You know where he is?"

Seth is sucking his smoke and staring at me. I can tell he's trying to decide whether to help me or slam the door in my face. I must look at least a little bit intimidating, or maybe he finally remembers me, because he shakes his head. "Luke moved out. Don't live here anymore."

Some guy, who I remember as Charlie, comes out of the kitchen. "Luke's living over Sunny's Bar now."

19

Great. Getting to Sunny's is going to take time—time Matt and Jules and I don't have. "Thanks," I mumble. I get out of there as quickly as I can, without even thinking about saying good-bye.

I haven't been to Sunny's before, but at least I know where it is. Sunny's is actually an old bar more toward the center of town, but the guy who owns it is another friend of my dad's. Who knows what Dad is doing there? Probably the exact same thing he was doing at the Lakeview apartment.

The bus trip to Sunny's seems long. I spend the whole time checking my watch and calculating the number of minutes I've been away from the hospital. I think way too hard. Has Matt noticed I left yet? What does he think of my leaving? Is Jules out of surgery yet? Needless to say, it's not a great ride.

Sunny's is one of the ugliest businesses I've ever seen. It looks like something out of a bad horror film, complete with peeling paint, a very brown lawn, and an old wooden sign missing half the letters that says SUN Y BAR and G IL. I wonder if the health department actually lets them serve food.

The inside of the place is dark too, mostly because half the light bulbs in it are burnt out. The tables are smeared with grease, and the bottles behind the bar are so dirty I could build Julia a sandbox with the crud caked onto them. I stop at the bar and wonder why the bartender doesn't look shocked to see a fourteen-year-old in front of him (and trust me, I don't look big for my age).

"Whatcha want, kid?"

I lean on the bar, trying to look a little more mature or something. Somehow, I don't think it's working. "Is Luke Porter here?"

That same look Seth gave me spreads across the bartender's face. He's trying to decide whether or not to help me.

"Maybe. Who are you?"

"His son."

He doesn't say anything else. He just turns and leaves the bar, and I follow him down a dusty hallway and up some stairs to a scratched and worn door. "Luke, some kid's here to see you. Says he belongs to you."

I force myself into the room. It's a mess of old green rugs, with little lighting, furniture, or color. It smells like rotten eggs and dirty socks. A few men are sitting around the room smoking. It only takes a quick scan before I notice my dad lying across a patch of floor by a heating duct.

It's getting hard not to grimace whenever I see him. He looks just like Matt, with dark-brown hair and these really intense bright-green eyes, and he used to be incredibly built when I was younger. Not anymore. He gets skinnier every time I see him these days. His hair is patchier around the back, and his teeth are starting to turn brown.

"Dusty!" He gets up quickly and comes over for a hug. "God I've missed you! What are you doing here?" They're both weird sentences to hear from your father when he's living in the same town as you, but I don't bother softening up the edges.

"Dad, Mom's not around and Julia's in the hospital. Her appendix burst."

He steps away from me. "Where did she go this time? Does she think she can just keep leaving you guys like that? Did you tell her to leave, Dusty?"

I shake my head, not too surprised that he missed the part about his daughter being in the hospital. He's not always all that sharp, my dad. "Dad, did you hear me? Julia's in the hospital. I need you to come with me."

Dad runs his hands through his thinning hair and sinks back onto a stained couch. "Geez, Dusty. She's in the hospital? Is it serious?"

How can it take so long for someone to digest something? I suck in a deep breath. "Yes, Dad, it's serious. The doctors want a parent there… you or Mom. They say Julia will be okay, but if you don't come back with me, they're going to start to wonder where you guys are."

21

I can see him mulling this over, and I take a second we don't have to wonder how it's possible I can look so little like this man. I don't look anything like my mom, either.

There's actually this picture of my family that a friend of my mom's took when Julia was just a baby. In it, Dad is standing behind Matt, and you can see how much they look alike—Matt has always had Dad's dark hair and green eyes. Mom is holding baby Julia, who already is a mini version of her with blond hair and brown eyes. I'm standing between Mom and Dad, the odd man out with light-brown hair and blue eyes, in the exact center of the picture—I look so different from them it's almost strange. I've never figured out who I'm supposed to look like.

"I can't come to the hospital with you, Dusty."

"What?" He says it so quietly I'm sure I must have heard him wrong.

"I said… I can't go with you. Not right now."

I've known since I left the hospital that this was a possibility. Isn't that the reason I've felt so anxious all evening? My dad has never been a real dad before, so why would he start now?

But to hear him say it, standing in front of me… to hear him sell us down the river without any real warning… to give us up without thinking about it for more than a second….

I almost take a swing at him. I want to. I can feel my fists clenching at my sides. I'm pretty sure the only thing that stops me is the fact that we're surrounded by guys who are a lot older and stronger than me. Maybe not, though. He is still my dad, and he's always looked so huge to me—even now, broom-handle skinny guy that he's become.

"You gotta understand, Dusty. I have deliveries to make; stuff to do. I can't just take off." He shakes his head. "Kid, I work with some guys who won't care why I left. They'll just care that I left. I mean, I'll come later, when I can. I just can't right now."

I just stare at him, incredulous. "Dad, what do you think it'll be like when I show up at the hospital with no parents? You don't think that will be bad? They'll put us into foster care, Dad."

"Dusty!" He shakes his head. "Don't be such a worrywart. It won't be like that. I'll be there eventually, or your mom will show up. She'll be back before they even notice anything is wrong."

And then he actually smiles at me.

He lives in a world all his own, that's for sure. As I look around that world, covered in grime and stain, I can't figure out why he likes this life so much better than the one with his kids.

I spin away from him and head for the door.

"Dusty—"

He doesn't get a chance to say anything else, though, because someone opens another door and start yelling, "Luke, you got packages ready in the other room."

I don't wait around to hear any more excuses. I just slam the door behind me.

I'm through Sunny's and outside again before my anger gives way to panic. What am I going to do? I have to go back to the hospital, and I have nothing to show for this trip of mine. No Dad, no Mom.

It's finally happened. After all that hard work… our cover's finally been blown.

I catch the bus, barely aware of what's going on around me. I think the bus driver asks me if I feel okay, but I don't really hear him. All I hear is my dad, over and over again, saying, "I can't go with you."

In my head I keep seeing that picture of the five of us. We'd all been at the park together. Mom had packed a picnic lunch, and she and her friend had sat on the grass with Julia while Dad and I played soccer and pretended to let Matt, who was really tiny then, play too. Mom's friend had taken the picture after we'd all gone for a walk around the lake together.

Too bad that's the only picture we have like that. That day was a total anomaly. My dad's never been the responsible-dad type. Even before he lost his job at the power plant and he and Mom broke up for good, he always drank too much and gambled all the time. Not exactly a shining role model.

I make a quick stop at home, just to see if my mother had a brain aneurysm that caused her to remember she has three kids and return home. No dice. The place is dark.

I go back to the hospital and stare at the entrance for a while before I can will myself to go in.

Nothing much has changed in the waiting room. Barbara is reading a book, Race is playing his Game Boy, and Matt is asleep on a couch. He looks so peaceful, so happy. I feel like I'm dealing him and Jules the biggest blow of their lives as I walk up to Barbara.

"Dusty!" She says it with immense, obvious relief. "You're back. Where's your mom?"

I didn't even hesitate this time. After all, what's left to do? Mom isn't going to reappear at any minute—she usually takes off for weeks at a time, and she's only been gone for a week and a half now—and my dad has made it perfectly clear where he stands.

The snow has been getting deeper and deeper, and it's now pretty clear I'm not going to make it up this mountain.

"Barbara? I need to talk to you."

JULIA IS in surgery for another hour. Matt spends the time sleeping and periodically waking up to watch cartoons again. Barbara gets some information from me about where Dad is, and I know she goes to talk to somebody about it, but we don't say much more about what's going to happen to us next. I don't really want to talk about it, so I don't ask. Race tries to do his homework and tries to get me to do mine too, but I can't concentrate on anything. When I tell him three plus five equals seven, he finally hands his Game Boy to me. "Oh, just play that," he says. "You're useless."

I can't do anything with that, either. All I can do is think. Where are we going to end up? Will they keep Julia and Matt together and make me disappear? Will that be my punishment for lying to everyone for so long? Finally I fall asleep across three cold, hard metal chairs. It is the worst place to take a nap, but I sleep like Matt after he's come off a Mountain Dew high until someone starts shaking my shoulder roughly. "Dusty, wake up." I hear Race call from what feels like a long way off. "Jules is out of surgery."

The room they have Jules in is small and cramped—Race says it's a recovery room. She looks smaller than I've ever seen her, her dirty-blond hair framing a face that is still really pale. At least she's sleeping. I pull a chair up next to her bed, and Matt quickly hops into my lap. We sit there for a moment, staring at her, with Race shadowing the doorway. Matt buries his head a little way into my shoulder. "She's going to be okay now, right Dusty?"

I can't answer that, so I don't.

# CHAPTER TWO

*FIVE YEARS Earlier*

"Mom, I need you to sign this."

*Dusty thrust the permission slip for the trip to the zoo in his mother's face. She was staring out the window at the mountains behind the apartment. "Not now, Dusty. I've had rough day."*

*Not again, thought Dusty. Just yesterday she'd been in a good enough mood to make cookies for Matt's preschool's holiday party and sing Julia to sleep. Dusty had known it couldn't last too long, but he'd been hoping it might last at least until after Christmas.*

*Matt came out of the bedroom in fire truck mode. "Woo-ooh, woo-ooh, woo-oh!" he shrieked as he raced around the room.*

*"Matthew!" Their mother whirled around. "Can you please shut up? I have a headache!"*

*Matt ran immediately to the big, strong, older brother who always gave him chocolate when Mom yelled. Sure enough, Dusty immediately led him toward the kitchen.*

*"Why is she mad again, Dusty?" Matt whimpered. "She wasn't mad yesterday."*

*Dusty wondered if maybe his mother talked to his dad. Ever since his dad stopped living with them all the time, she seemed worse whenever she talked to him. "Don't worry, Matt. We'll just leave her alone for awhile until her headache goes away."*

*From their bedroom, Dusty could hear the sounds of gurgling and spitting. Julia must have woken up, which meant she'd be hungry soon. He hoped his mom had at least remembered to buy baby food.*

*He sighed as he realized he'd have to feed Julia, probably. Whenever Mom got into moods like this she usually forgot Julia, leaving the baby in her crib for hours sometimes. Dusty thought it was good thing that Mom planned to put the baby into daycare soon. They'd probably take better care of her.*

*He opened the cabinet doors, looking for baby food before Julia could start crying for dinner. He hated it when Julia cried even more than he used to hate it when Matt cried.*

"IT'S GOING to take us a few days to look into all your options. Until then, we're releasing you into Barbara's custody."

The social worker has a soft voice, but it feels like her words are a fire poker coming toward my skin. Staying with Barbara is okay news—at least I'll get a few more days with Matt and Jules—but it makes things very clear where my living situation is now concerned.

"What about Dad?" I ask. "I know he's not here right now, but he's in town. I know where he is. I swear I do. Then you could talk to him yourself." Maybe she can convince him it's time to stop screwing around with his friends.

The social worker, whose name is Ms. Davies, tries to put her hand on top of mine. I pull my hand away, and she blows some loose strands of hair off her forehead. She is young, maybe only twenty-five, with short black hair and dark eyes. Most guys my age would probably say she's pretty good-looking, but she may as well have warts covering her face right then—she looks that ugly to me.

"Dusty, what your dad did… leaving you alone like that for so long…." She hesitates. "Dusty, that's a crime. It's called child

27

neglect. The police will be looking for him. When they find him, they will arrest him."

Ice runs through my body for a moment, and I can feel my hands forming fists. The room is turning black around the edges. "You can't do that," I manage to say. "We don't care. We're just fine. He always gives us money." I turn to Barbara, looking desperately for a way out of this situation. "If I'd known that would happen, I wouldn't have told you anything." I can hear my voice getting darker and sharper, until it doesn't even sound like it belongs to me anymore.

Barbara nods. "I know, Dusty," she says quietly. I half-expect her to try to hug me, but she stays put.

"So we stay with Barbara, then? For how long? Until you find my mom? Or is she going to get arrested too?" Ms. Davies doesn't answer that; she doesn't need to. I already know the answer. If Dad has neglected us, Mom certainly has too.

"Dusty, you'll stay with Barbara until I'm able to look into all the best options for you and your siblings. We'll be checking with any relatives you have and looking into foster care."

Foster care. The ice in my body that had thawed when I learned we'd be staying with Barbara refreezes, and I can feel myself tense up again. We don't have any close relatives that I know of. My parents don't have any brothers or sisters, and all our grandparents are dead. "If we go into foster care, we'll get split up, won't we?"

Ms. Davies starts to reach for my hand again, but she quickly stops. "We'll do our best not to do that, Dusty. I promise I'll try everything I can."

I'm not really in the habit of trusting adults, so that sentence doesn't mean a whole lot to me.

The doctor tells us that Julia's going to be in the hospital for at least another day, and I want to stay with her, so Barbara ends up taking Matt home with her and Race that night so he can get some sleep. I curl up on a lounge chair one of the nurses brings in for me and wait for Julia to wake up. She looks so peaceful, sound asleep like that. I'm afraid of what I'll say to her when she finally breaks back into consciousness.

How am I going to tell her and Matt that I finally lost them? I start absent-mindedly putting those words together in my head, trying to find phrasings I can use. *Guys, we're going to be apart for awhile. We'll still see each other all the time.* Just thinking about it is giving me a pounding headache, and I'm starting to pace the room when I heard a teeny voice whisper. "Dusty?"

I race over to Julia's bedside. "Hey." I grin. "You're awake."

Julia is staring blankly at the white walls surrounding her. It's pretty obvious she's terrified. "It's okay," I tell her. "You're in the hospital. They had to take your appendix out."

Julia's eyes go round. "What's a pendick?"

At least that makes me smile; it's so good to hear her voice again. "Just a part of you that you don't need anymore. Don't worry. I'm right here with you, and you'll be able to leave soon."

Julia nods. "And we can go home?"

I hesitate slightly. We'll probably never go back to our old apartment again, and I know it. "Not right away, Jules." I breathe a sigh of relief when she doesn't ask why. She just curls up and starts sucking her thumb. Once again, I don't try to stop her.

I WAKE up groggy and disoriented, uncertain where I am. It takes me a few minutes to register everything that has gone on in the last twenty-four hours or so; a quick recap of those events has me wide awake in no time.

Julia's already awake and picking at a bowl of Jell-O someone left for her. "Hey, Julia," I say. "How are you feeling?"

Julia frowns. "My tummy still hurts a little," she says with incredible concentration, "but I'm not tired anymore."

"Good." I start over toward her bed and am sitting on the edge of it when Matt comes rushing in.

"Julia, you're awake!" He comes running over to hug her, and she puts down her dish for a moment to hug him back. I see her wince a little as he grabs her, so I pull him away gently. "Calm down, chief. She's still a little sick."

Julia frowns at me. "I am not," she says smartly. "Matt, do you want some of my Jell-O?" He starts slurping it down with her, telling her all about Race's house. "He has these really cool video games, and he let me play some last night!" I'm staring at them, wistfully thinking about how close they really are. I wonder if they'll get split up too. I only have a second to think about that before Barbara comes in.

"Hey, Dusty," she says. She tries to pat me on the shoulder, but I hop off the bed and step out of the way. "I just dropped Race off at school and let them know what was going on. They said they'd make up an assignment package for what you're missing." I just shrug. Who really cares about school anymore? Now that I don't have to put on the Golden Child front anymore, there doesn't seem much point in getting good grades. Not to mention that I probably won't even be going to Prescott for much longer.

The kids keep rambling about video games and Jell-O, and Barbara sinks into the chair I slept in the night before. "Listen, Dusty, you should probably know that Ms. Davies called. She wants to meet me this morning in a few hours, and she said it would probably be best that you attended."

I'm instantly wary. *She's found homes for us already,* I think. *Great.* "Who'll watch the kids?"

Barbara looks over at them, a distant smile on her face. "Oh, I asked around the nurses' station. There's a nurse who thinks they are just adorable, and she said she'd keep an eye on them."

So this is it—the moment of truth. Ms. Davies is going to tell us we'll be going to separate places. There is no way I am going to let that happen; not after all the work I've put into making sure we stay a family. I start making back-up plans in my head. *Can I run away with Matt and Julia? Hide out at the old apartment until the rent money runs out? Nah, that's the first place they'll look for us. Maybe if I take the kids with me and go see Dad again....* I spend the next few hours adding details to far-fetched plans I'll never be able to pull off. Matt and Julia start playing Candy Land together. At least Julia seems okay, especially for a kid who just had surgery the day before.

Around ten o'clock, Barbara goes to find the nurse who offered to watch the kids. Once Julia and Matt have safely pulled the poor woman into their amazingly long Candy Land tournament, Barbara signals to me that it's time for the meeting.

Ms. Davies is seated at a long table in a large conference room. She has on a black suit and large gold earrings, and she suddenly looks a lot more menacing than she did the day before. The room is so tense that it feels like we're facing off in some kind of battle. Well, I guess we kind of are. Teenager vs. Department of Children and Families. They definitely have the advantage in this one. Dad's bookies probably wouldn't even give me 50:1 odds.

"Dusty," she smiles. "How are you holding up?"

I try to give her the hardest look I have. It's the same look I gave the guy at Sunny's the day before. "Okay." I shrug. "Julia seems to be fine."

"Good." She opens a manila file folder in front of her. "Well, Dusty, I have big news. I started off by looking to see if you had any living relatives within the states. I managed to come up with something interesting. Dusty, were you aware your mother had an older brother?"

I blink a few times in rapid succession. Mom has always told me she's an only child. "No way," I say with a frown.

"Yes, apparently he lives in Danville, Vermont—your mother's hometown. His name is Jackson Morton."

I open my mouth to say something, but nothing comes out. Jackson is my middle name.

"He's married to a woman named Beth. Apparently they have no children, but they have always wanted to. Mr. Morton was quite shocked to hear you and your brother and sister existed. He said he's had no contact with your mother since she left Vermont at the age of eighteen. Jack and Beth would like very much for all three of you to go live with them."

It's one of those moments when you know something is coming, but you somehow hold out hope that it won't arrive. Maybe, you think, it will take a detour or something—or get hit by a truck, or some bad weather will hold it up. Well, this sentence doesn't encounter any of those problems, and now I'm staring down the idea of moving clear across the country. "When?"

Ms. Davies looks into her file folder. "Your aunt and uncle had actually already started the paperwork to become foster parents at some point in the future, so it shouldn't take us too long to okay them as your guardians." She closes the folder and looks back up. "If they check out okay, and it looks like they will, they'd like to come out and meet you guys within a few weeks."

Barbara and Ms. Davies start talking rapidly, and I take a few deep breaths. Long-lost relatives and moving to Vermont. Not things I've been expecting. I don't want to be in this cramped, tense room anymore, so I take off out of there as quickly as I can. I don't even know where I am going; I'm just headed anywhere that isn't that room.

"Dusty!" I can hear Barbara calling behind me. "Dusty, come back!"

"I'm going to Jules's room!" I yell back down the hallway. Doctors and nurses are looking at me strangely, and I soon realize that's because Barbara is chasing me down the hallway. She grabs my shoulder, forcibly turning me around.

"Dusty," she heaves, out of breath, "I'm sorry all this is happening. But you need to understand, this is a good thing!"

"Really? A good thing?" It's hard to tone down the sarcasm in my voice. "You think my brother and sister and I getting shipped halfway across the country to live with complete strangers is a good thing? You've got a strange idea of what makes something stellar news."

"Dusty," she says with a frown, "don't you understand how serious this situation is? How close you and Julia and Matt came to being split up and placed with different families? Especially you! You're already in high school. Ms. Davies was talking about putting you into a group home."

"Serious? Serious?" I realize I'm yelling, but I don't care. "Do I know how serious this is? Who's been washing clothes and doing dishes and making endless cups of ramen for years now? Who's been lying to the Prescott secretaries constantly and begging his dad for money just to keep *that woman*—" Here I pause and gesture frantically down the hallway toward Ms. Davies. "—out of their life? Yeah, Barbara," I tell her, "I think I know how serious this is."

She looks at me strangely. "Then why aren't you at least a little bit happy about this?"

I remember, right after I met Race, wishing my mother was more like his. At this moment I wish I'd never seen her stupid face. I glare at her. "I'm not…. I don't know, okay? I don't want to move across the country. I don't want an aunt or an uncle." I practically hiss that part through my teeth. "We would've been fine if you hadn't told anybody about my parents. But you had to go tell everybody what was going on."

She purses her lips. "You're darn right I did, Dusty," she says quietly. I can't keep my glare going, so I turn back to walk toward Julia's room. Barbara doesn't say another word, but I can feel her behind me the whole way there.


HOURS LATER, Race and I are sitting in the cafeteria drinking sodas and eating really bad cake. His mom dropped him off after school so he could keep me company while Julia sleeps. She took Matt home with her so he could get some rest and do some homework. She didn't even ask me if I wanted to go back to their house. I think she already knew that answer. I would've rather had Matt not go anywhere near her either, but I couldn't ask him to stay at the hospital all night with me.

"So you guys are moving to Vermont," Race says quietly. He is definitely not his usual self. He's pushing the chocolate icing in front of him around his plate in big circles, and he keeps almost tipping his soda over with his elbow and grabbing it at the last minute.

I shrug. "Just until I figure something out. Not forever," I add hastily.

Race shrugs. "Well, maybe it'll be good."

"Whaddya mean?" I can feel my eyes narrowing. "What do you think could ever be good about us moving?" For the second time in two days, my vision of Race blurs.

"I dunno…." Race's eyes shift. "I mean, maybe now you'll have time to skateboard and do what you want and you won't have to be with Julia and Matt all the time. Maybe you'll have… you know… parents."

I can't believe what I'm hearing. "I have parents," I snort. "What's wrong with you anyway? I thought you'd be all pissed at your mom for ratting us out and getting me sent to Vermont, but it sounds like you're taking her side."

Now Race's eyes are beginning to narrow. "She didn't have a choice, Dusty," he says. "I mean, what was she supposed to do? Not say anything?"

"Well, it's not like you ever told her what was going on!" I can't quite believe Race is going along with all this.

"'Course I didn't, stupid," he says. "I knew she'd have to tell people. Duh. Dusty, you are really stupid sometimes. In the real world," he goes on sarcastically, "normal people make sure that kids have parents." He makes sure to put extra emphasis on the phrase "real world."

I stand quickly, feeling my head spin. "You know," I say loudly, not caring who else in the cafeteria can hear me, "maybe leaving this place won't matter so much. It's not like I had any friends here or anything."

"Whatever, Dusty." Race stands too, flipping his hair out of his face. "You think whatever you wanna think. We both know my mom had to do what she did. You couldn't keep doing what you were doing, even if you never admit it." He storms out of the cafeteria.

I just stand there, staring stupidly at the chocolate cake still on the tray, wishing I could chuck it into the wall.

And the whole time, I know it doesn't matter what I do anymore. My future's being laid out for me now.

It kind of makes me wonder if Zeb wanted to turn back on that trek up the peak, or if his team made him change course. Was he the kind of guy who would have died conquering the mountain? Was it the people around him who made him give it up and head back to safety?

And if it wasn't his idea, could he have made it up if they just would have let him try?


"DUSTY, WHAT if they don't like me?"

It's four days later, and Matt, Jules, and I are sitting in the basement office of Barbara's house. Skype is up on the computer screen in front of me, and Julia's worried that the random faces about to appear there won't like us.

You ever have one of those moments where you actually can't believe what's happening is really happening?

I lift Julia onto my lap. "'Course they'll like you. Everyone does. And if they don't, I won't let us move there."

Matt is sitting next to us, not saying anything. He's been strangely silent about all this since I told him and Julia about our new relatives a few days ago—he just sort of nodded and asked me a few questions about Vermont. Julia, on the other hand, hasn't shut up. It's been all, "Is Mom coming too?" "Can I bring my toys?" "Will my school be there?"

If I really didn't want to meet this new aunt and uncle, I'd be almost happy about this Skype session—finally, someone besides Barbara to help with all the questions.

The computer makes a weird, almost gurgly, sound. "What's that?" Julia asks.

"Uh…." I'm not so great with a lot of computer stuff. We've never owned our own, so I pretty much only know how to do whatever I learned at school or messing around with Race's laptop.

Matt rolls his eyes. "It's them calling, duh," he says, and he leans over to click a button with the mouse.

I nudge him. "Show-off."

And then two faces are suddenly filling the screen in front of us, and I know right away they're our aunt and uncle.

Jack is, like, a mirror image of me. He has my brown hair, my blue eyes, the same nose, even the same skinnier body type as me— he's just got a little more muscle. All my life I've wondered why I don't look like either Mom or Dad, and now I'm pretty sure I know the reason Mom gave me Jack's name. Maybe I've always looked exactly like her brother.

"Hi, guys," he says, and I realize we even sound a lot alike. "I'm your Uncle Jack, and this is your Aunt Beth."

"Hello." The woman next to him smiles. She's nice-looking enough, with dark hair and eyes, and a huge smile stretched all the way across her face.

None of the three of us say anything. I'm still trying to get some sort of greeting out of my mouth when Julia waves at the screen.

"Hi! I'm Julia, but my brothers call me Jules sometimes."

Matt shrugs at me and starts talking. "I'm Matt," he says. He glances at the room behind them, which is full of fancy-looking furniture. "Your house looks nice."

Beth's face lights up. "I'm so glad you like it! We were going to carry around the laptop later and give you a tour, if you'd like that."

Matt looks intrigued. "Sure."

I know it's coming, but I'm still caught off guard when the two of them turn to me next. Jack grins, and I know he is thinking of how much we look alike. "You must be Dustin."

"Dusty," says Julia, suddenly grabbing my hand. It's amazing how much strength that quickly gives me. "Yeah," I add, clearing my throat. "Everybody calls me Dusty."

"Hello, Dusty." Beth smiles at me widely. "I'm very glad to meet you."

I can't seem to return the smile, so I just nod.

THE REST of the conversation goes pretty well. We find out they have two dogs, and that gets Matt all excited—he's always wanted a dog. Jack asks me what courses I'm taking in school; turns out he's a math teacher at the high school I'll go to out there. Great. Just what I need. Beth starts telling us that she and Jack are going to fly out soon to meet us, and that they're really excited. They've been to Colorado before, but never Colorado Springs, so Julia and Matt start telling them about it.

I don't say much. Mostly just nod here and there.

It's the end of the conversation, though, that gets to me, even though it's the part that definitely makes Julia and Matt pretty happy. That's when Jack and Beth decide to give us a "virtual tour" of our new home.

They start off by taking the laptop to the kitchen. It's definitely an older house. The kitchen has ancient-looking light fixtures, and the floors are a dark, bowed hardwood. It is nice, though. Comforting. It's colored in reds and browns, and it looks as though someone has put a lot of thought into it.

Then we watch the screen as Beth walks through the dining room, which is all green, and into a huge blue living room with tons of electronics and two soft, comfy-looking sofas. I'm a little in awe of the large television. "Wow!" says Matt. "You guys must watch a lot of TV!"

Beth starts laughing. "You'd think that, wouldn't you? But we hardly ever watch any at all. Jack just likes electronics. He buys anything he thinks looks cool." She shows us the downstairs bathroom, Jack's study, which is where they were just talking to us, and the laundry room.

The she carries the laptop upstairs.

"I want you to keep in mind that it's only been a few days, so all the bedrooms aren't done yet." All the bedrooms? Are we each getting our own? Matt and I have always shared a room, and when Julia was younger we'd had an even smaller apartment and the three of us shared one. I've never had a room of my own. I've always wondered what Race did with a room all to himself.

The upstairs hallway is long. I count three doors on either side of it. Beth opens the first one on the right. "Julia, this will be your room," she says. "You uncle Jack and I sleep right across the hall." The door swings out, and my mouth falls open.

The whole room is painted pink with purple trim. The walls are already decorated with pictures of puppies, kittens, and little kids laughing and playing. The bed is entirely pink, and a row of Barbies lay across the pillow as if they're waiting for Jules. "I love it! I love it! I love it!" Julia shrieks, grabbing at the computer screen as if she could walk right through it and into the room.

"How'd you know…?" I ask, clearing my throat. "How'd you know about the pink?"

Beth turns the laptop so she can wink at me. "I have my ways."

I am now even more curious what our rooms are going to look like. Matt's room is, not too surprisingly, decorated entirely with soccer stuff. There's soccer-ball wallpaper, pictures of famous players on the walls, even soccer-ball pillows. Matt starts jumping up and down, clapping his hands. "You knew I like soccer! How'd you know?" he shouts.

I was worried about how he'd take the news that we wouldn't be sharing a room anymore, but it looks like he's going to be just fine on his own.

Beth moves the computer out of Matt's room and points it down the hallway as we walk. "That's the bathroom, that's the guest room...." She stops at the last door in hallway. "Dusty, Jack and I weren't sure where you'd want to live, but Jack said teenage boys like their space, so we thought we'd give you that tower room. What do you think?"

Space? What did I need with space? And the tower room? Was it going to be far away from everyone else? "I don't really care," I mutter.

"We'll just see if you like it, then." She pulls open a door, and then the computer's heading up a winding flight of stairs. It seems darker than the rest of the house, but at the top of the stairs light streams in from the windows that circle a bed, small desk, dark bureau, and armchair. There isn't any special wallpaper or anything, though. The room is painted a light blue, with dark-blue trim. It's okay.

Beth's talking again. "I couldn't seem to find out what your favorite color was. So I figured, blue?"

I don't say anything, and Beth turns the laptop again. This time I can see her and Jack.

"You know," Beth starts slowly, "this room used to belong to your mother."

Julia gasps with delight. "Mom lived there?"

"Of course. This was your grandparents' house. Jack thought one of you might want your mom's old room.... Of course, it wasn't always blue."

I don't have anything else to say, so I decide to go with the obvious. "Thanks."

# CHAPTER THREE

*FOUR YEARS Earlier*

*"Dusty, where's Mom?"*

*Dusty woke to find Matt staring at him. "What do you mean, Matt?"*

*"I want breakfast. She's not in bed."*

*Dusty tried to shake the sleep from his eyes. "What are you talking about, Matt?"*

*Matt threw off Dusty's covers and grabbed his hand, frustrated. "I mean she's not in bed! I can't find her."*

*Uh-oh. Their mom had gone out with a friend the night before, promising Dusty she'd be home no later than midnight. Dusty had tried to stay up to wait for her, but he'd fallen asleep around one thirty.*

*Lately, their mom had been having more and more of her "moods." Twice that week Dusty had taken Matt and Julia to daycare himself because their mother wouldn't get out of bed. She even lost another job.*

*Dusty followed Matt to their mother's bedroom which, sure enough, was empty. "Uh.... I bet she just stayed out too late and decided to sleep over at Aunt Sammy's, Matt." Dusty winced at Sammy's name. He actually hated calling the woman his aunt. She was too loud and always patted Dusty on the head when she saw him. He hated that. Still, Mom insisted they call her Aunt Sammy.*

*Matt started to pout, and Dusty could hear Julia yelling from the next room. "Mommy!"*

Okay, *Dusty thought,* I can do this. *Get them some cereal, get them to the daycare. No big deal.*

*As long as Mom was home by the time they got home from school that afternoon, it wouldn't be a big deal at all.*

"DUSTY, MY ears feel weird."

I pull a piece of Juicy Fruit out of my pocket and hand it to Matt. "Here, chew this."

He pops it into his mouth and leans back into his seat. "That's better," he says through the gum. "Hey, why'd that work?"

I smile. "Don't worry about it, kiddo. Read a book until you can play that Game Boy Jack gave you." Any other time, I'd probably enjoy explaining altitude pressure and all that stuff to him, but right now I have too much other stuff on my mind. Julia fell asleep across my lap before takeoff, or no doubt she'd still be asking questions too. The last few hours have been nothing but "When are we getting to Beth's house? How are we getting there again?"

It's pretty obvious Jack and Beth have already won her over. They've come out to see us in Colorado Springs since we first talked to them on the computer, and Julia can't seem to get enough of them. Matt's pretty much in too at this point—Jack's got him all excited about playing soccer there, and I'm sure the Game Boy helped. Jack and Beth have both spent a lot of time asking what I'm into, but I just responded with a whole lot of shrugging. I'm not falling for that. The kids may be too young to recognize bribery, but I'm not. At some point Barbara caved and told them I really like skateboarding, but when they asked me about it, I told them I don't skateboard anymore.

41

It's not totally a lie. I haven't skateboarded since Race and I stopped talking to each other after that fight in the hospital.

And believe me, it's not easy to stay not speaking to someone you're staying in the same house with. Barbara tried a bunch of times to get us talking again, but neither of us was having it.

I sigh, running everything that's happened in the past few weeks over in my head. Jack and Beth are definitely nice enough, but the fact that they've been decent doesn't make me want to move to Vermont any more than I used to. I'm really glad we're doing this trip on our own. They offered to fly back out again to "bring us home," as Beth put it, but I asked if we could just fly out there by ourselves. I wanted one last chance for it to be the three of us, I guess.

I went through five or six drafts of plans to run away with the kids and bring them to see Dad before I finally realized that wasn't going to get me anything except maybe time in juvie. Dad was the problem here, not the solution. He'd been right there in Colorado Springs, a bus ride away from stopping this plane trip, and I hadn't even been able to convince him to come see his daughter in the hospital. It would be a tough contest who I hate more right now: Dad, or the entire social services department of the state of Colorado.

Or Mom. The woman hasn't even bothered to show her face in the weeks since Julia got out of the hospital. Knowing Mom, she probably heard what was going on with us and made herself scarce rather than risk getting arrested. I haven't been all that surprised; by now I've gotten pretty used to being sold out by my own parents.

But even if I'm not really going to miss them, there are plenty of things I'm sorry to say good-bye to. Prescott, the school I'd been going to for the last ten years. Friends (besides Race) that I've known since I was five, even if I've never known them all that well. Pikes Peak too. I shake my head, like I'm trying to get the memories of the Springs to fall out of my head or something. Even though I know you can't really do that, I'm pretty sure I have to try to put Colorado behind me. No use lingering over things you're leaving behind. As we'd left Colorado, the Front Range Mountains had stared me down through the window of the airport. I'd realized then that home is mostly the scenery you know and the people who matter to you. Leaving them both at the same time can be treacherous if you dwell on it too long.

The man next to me starts shifting in his seat uncomfortably, so I move Julia around in my lap to give him a little more room. They sure don't give you a heck of a lot of space in economy class.

"Thanks," he nods, adjusting his tie. He's a young black guy, tall, and he looks all business in a gray suit and shiny shoes. His tie has some diamond-looking pattern on it. "Those your brother and sister?" he asks, gesturing toward Matt and Jules.

We've reached cruising altitude, and Matt is totally engrossed in his video game. At least he's plugged headphones into it so the beeping won't bug the other passengers. Jules is still completely unconscious. "Yeah. They're usually a lot more... aware of what's going on, though."

He chuckles at that. "Bet it'll make your flight a lot easier. Are you traveling alone?"

I stare at the seat in front of me. "Yeah, we are. We're going to see our aunt and uncle."

"They live in New York?"

I'd forgotten that's where our stopover is. "Nah, upstate Vermont. Are you from New York?" I glance over at him.

"Brooklyn all the way." He smiles. I thought his accent sounded funny. "I was just at a conference in Colorado Springs. It's got some impressive views. Is that where you live?"

The guy has no idea what a loaded question he's just asked. Suddenly I'm sorry I ever started a conversation with him. "Yeah," I mumble. "At least, we used to. Maybe not anymore."

He must realize that isn't the best question to ask, because he doesn't say anything for a few minutes after that. I'm more than happy to end the conversation on that note and go back to staring stupidly at the seat in front of me, but at some point he clears his throat and starts speaking again.

"You know," he says quietly, "I actually grew up with my aunt and uncle."

This is already starting to sound suspiciously like one of those "I got through it and you'll get through it too" pep talks adults like to give. I definitely am not in the mood for one of those, and I don't even know this guy. "So?" I say nastily.

He just shrugs. I guess you can't throw a guy from Brooklyn off that easily. "So it sucked for awhile." He looks me in the eye. "But it always sucked less than living with my mom."

I glance over Julia and Matt to make sure they aren't listening to any of this. Jules is still out, and Matt is still living in his new Game Boy. I decide to be blunt. "What was wrong with your mom?"

"Oh, she just loved heroin a little too much. My aunt decided to take me off her hands."

Is this guy being honest? Do people lie about that kind of stuff? "Does that mean I'm supposed to tell you what's wrong with my parents?"

He smirks. "Doesn't mean anything, except that's the story. I could care less what you tell me."

I believe him, and I suddenly I don't care either. What does it matter? Matt and Julia aren't listening, and I'll probably never see this guy again as long as I live. "Our dad's messed up on drugs too, I think. He's gone a lot. Our mom's gone pretty often too. Maybe doing drugs. I don't know."

"But your aunt and uncle want you to live with them. Are you okay with that?"

I choke on my gum. "You're pretty nosy, you know that?"

"Hey, I just ask questions. I travel a lot, and flights get boring with no one to talk to. You don't have to answer anything."

I wait about a minute before I decide to answer. "It just bugs me, you know? What's Vermont like? I've never been there. I never even knew I had an aunt and uncle." I pause. "You know, I have

44

dreams of my mom showing up to drag the kids and me out of this mess. She always looks surprised in the dream. 'I wasn't arrested. Don't be silly, Dusty,' she always says. They're just dreams, though. I know it's stupid."

"Just your mom? You don't dream about your dad doing that?"

I scowled at the seat. "Guess not," I mutter.

"You do want to be back with your mom, then."

I snort incredulously. "Not really. That woman's a basket case, and I can't really stand her either. But if she was around again, things would go back to the way they used to be. When my parents weren't around, I always took care of them"—I gesture toward Matt and Julia—"just fine. We don't need these relatives. I can handle my brother and sister just fine."

"What do they think of the whole thing?" The guy, whose name I have just realized I still don't know, glances over at Jules and Matt.

"They're okay with it," I say begrudgingly.

"Really? They won't miss your parents at all?" The guy is talking again.

"Nah. I guess...." I think about how excited Julia has been to have Beth cooing over her and buying her dolls, and I stare wistfully at her blond hair; it's right from our mom. "There isn't much for them to miss."

"If it helps...." I don't think it will, but I let the guy go on. "I had a little brother, too. Only he and I were really close to the same age, and neither of us wanted to live anywhere without our mom. We hated our aunt and uncle for about a year. Then...."

"What?" Maybe he'll say his mom got her act together and came to rescue them.

"I started to really like it." He crosses his arms and looks me in the eye again. "I liked having someone to cook dinner. Do the laundry. Come to my parent conferences at school. Listen to me when I had a good day, or a bad day... or any day."

45

That isn't what I expected—or wanted—to hear. "Maybe. Still, I can do all that for my brother and sister. I do now anyway."

"Well, sure," he replies, "but who does it for you?"

That startles me, and it takes me a minute to respond. "I don't need anyone to do that for me. I'm just fine, thanks." I'm being sarcastic, but I don't care.

He glances me up and down. "How old are you? Thirteen?"

"Fourteen. Almost fifteen."

He shakes his head. "Just my age," I hear him mumble. "Well, kid, whatever you want to believe. But I think you just might change your mind." He hands me a business card. It says JED DAVIES: PUBLIC RELATIONS on it in large letters. "My name's Jed Davies. That's my cell phone on there."

"Why are you giving me this?" I ask, probably a little snottily.

He shrugs. "You know, I have no idea. I just think I'd like to see how this whole thing works out for you."

I shove the card into my pocket, fully intending to toss it in the first trash can I see, and we don't talk the rest of the flight. Every now and then Jed looks over at us and smiles and shakes his head, but I don't care what he does or thinks. What does he know? Just because things worked out for him, what makes him think they'll work out for us?

I spend the rest of the flight tensely watching the TV screen hanging from the ceiling of the airplane, wondering what Beth and Jack will be like. Not that it will matter much to me anyway. I know I don't need them, even if everybody else seems to think I do.

We switch planes in New York. Julia is barely conscious through the whole thing, and Matt only turns his video game off long enough for landing and the new takeoff. Jed nods to me as we step off the plane, but neither of us says good-bye. Julia instantly goes back to sleep on our new flight and finally wakes up as the plane touches ground in Burlington, Vermont, which gives me an odd feeling of relief. A pressure is suddenly sitting in my chest, and it isn't from the change in altitude. I'm glad I don't have to spend time coaxing Jules awake.

As the aisle of the plane fills with travelers anxious to get off, I pull our heavy jackets out of the overhead compartment and help Julia into hers. It is mid-October, and Jack has told us over and over again it will already be very cold in Northern Vermont, even colder than Colorado Springs. He and Beth took us shopping for better winter stuff on their last visit.

The airport is pretty small, and there is no tunnel connecting the plane to the airport, so the kids and I walk down the airplane steps and onto the landing strip. Jack was right; it is colder here. I mean, Colorado Springs isn't exactly summer all year round. Still, this cold is different somehow... more biting. It chills me straight through, something the cold in Colorado Springs never quite did. I check to make sure Matt and Julia have their jackets zipped, and we follow the crowd of passengers into the airport, where waiting friends and family are lined up behind a bar separating incoming passengers from the airport lobby.

I glance right to left, and of course Beth and Jack are right there waiting for us. Jack pulls Julia up into his arms for a hug before passing her to Beth, and Matt easily lets them both gather him against their legs for hugs as well. Jack just reaches out to shake my hand. The last time they left he tried to hug me, and I stepped away. Looks like he's not trying again.

After we get our luggage off the turnstile and begin to head through the airport, Julia starts to lag back a little. I pull the backpack off my back and lean down so I can give her a piggyback ride. She's starting to climb on when Jack sweeps her up to carry her. "I've got her, Dusty. You must be exhausted." Beth is holding onto Matt's hand, so I drop back behind them as we finish the walk out of the airport.

Outside, the wet, frigid air brushes around us again, and I shiver even though I'm trying not to. I look around me for the first time, and I'm surprised to find mountains rolling their way around the scenery, in every shade of orange and yellow and red you can

47

possibly imagine. They're nothing like the mountains in Colorado Springs. Those are tall and intimidating, and they start and stop abruptly. These are shorter, more approachable, but they seem to go on forever. I wonder where they end up, and if anybody like Zeb Pike has ever tried to climb them and failed. Unlikely. These mountains are much shorter than Pikes Peak; good old Zeb could have conquered one of them easily.

The ride from Burlington to Danville takes about forty minutes. I kind of listen to Beth tell us about what we're driving past, which seem to range from covered bridges to small stores to one of the only two malls in half the state. Nothing very exciting. The entire landscape is wrapped in those same bright oranges and yellows I first noticed, and anything that isn't, like the grass, is a sort of mud-brown color. Lots of trees have already lost their leaves, and they look pretty dank and depressing. The sky is a dark gray, and Jack and Beth both mention that it might snow any day now. "It often snows before Halloween," Beth adds.

"It does that in Colorado sometimes too," Matt puts in from the backseat.

"Not this year!" Julia responds. "It's been warm. This year Dusty said I could probably wear my costume without a jacket as long as it stays warm."

Jack glances at me in the rearview mirror, but I just shrug. I don't much feel like explaining Colorado's notoriously unpredictable weather patterns, or telling Julia that her hopes of a costume without a coat were probably shot the moment we stepped off that airplane. I'm not too happy about leaving Colorado's currently warm weather anyway. You can't skateboard in the snow.

"How tall are the mountains?" I ask at one point.

Jack chuckles. "They're probably nothing compared to the Colorado peaks you're used to, Dusty. They tend to cap out at a little over four thousand feet."

He's right. That is nothing like what I'm used to. Still, even these mountains seem impressive somehow. It's too bad they're so… different.

48

"...And this is Colby High School, where I teach, where Dusty will go to school." We're driving through a small downtown area, full of small stores with names like "Jen's Diner" and "Pat's Dress Palace." The high school Jack points out is huge, though, with at least three wings. It's older than any building I've ever seen in Colorado. The front is dark brick, and it's covered in ivy from top to bottom.

"It's pretty big for such a small town," I mutter. I don't even realize Jack is listening to me, but he nods from the driver's seat. "It's what's called a regional high school. This is actually the town of Colby, but they take in students from all the surrounding towns, including Danville. Most of the towns around here are too small to have their own high school."

I'm thinking about that when I realize something huge. "Wait, you mean Jules and Matt will go to a different school than I will?"

Beth turns in her seat. "Of course. They'll go to the elementary school in Danville. I thought we already told you that?"

I guess they probably did, but I'm sure I wasn't paying much attention. I've never really thought about what schools we'll go to. I haven't ever been to a different school from the kids—I started going to Prescott long before either one of them was old enough to go to school, back when Mom was having a "good mom" moment and was pretty intent on making sure her kids got a good education. She visited Prescott, chose it herself, and even moved us a few miles across town so we could be down the street from it. One of my favorite activities was bringing Matt and Julia back and forth to Prescott every day. The idea of not spending every morning and afternoon with them is... well, disturbing.

My look probably turns dark, but nobody seems to notice. Jack starts talking about all the great things Julia and Matt are going to get to do at Danville Elementary, and I sort of check out of the conversation. I stare out the window, the strange, new mountains staring back at me, and I wonder how I am ever going to begin to like this place.

Jack and Beth's house is in the middle of nowhere, spread out against the background of a giant, brown-and-green field. The neighbors are at least a mile apart on each side. It's a huge old Victorian, red with white trim. There's even a little tower leaning out of the right-hand side of the frame. My room, I'm pretty sure. Next to the house itself is a smaller building that looks like it used to be a shed. A raised blue sign above the door of the building reads "Morton Real Estate."

"Real estate?" I look at Jack. "I thought you were a teacher."

Jack parks the car in the driveway and Beth starts to open the door. "The real estate business is mine," she says. "It's very well-established. I even managed to arrange things so I could take some time off this week and get you guys settled." She opens up the back door and starts to help Julia out, brushing Julia's hair back at the same time. Nope, it isn't my imagination—she really does look at Julia like she's a doll just waiting to be dressed up.

Matt jumps out of the car and quickly surveys the area. I can practically feel his eyes boring into the giant backyard, the brown fields stretching out from behind the house, the neighbor's house far down the road. "Hey, where're the dogs?" he calls out.

Jack puts his hand on Matt's shoulder. "Don't worry, kiddo. You won't be able to miss 'em once we get into the house."

Jack's right. The second we step into the front door, we're surrounded by loud barking. A golden lab and smaller dog that looks like a mutt come charging at us, paws raised. Julia squeals and buries her head in my jacket, and for the first time since we arrived in Vermont, I relax a little.

"Get away, you crazy dogs!" Jack hollers, pushing past us. "The big lab is Missy; the other one's name is Portia."

"Portia," Matt says quietly. He approaches the dogs slowly, but he doesn't need to. Portia immediately comes running up to lick his hand.

Jack ushers us in past the dogs. "C'mon, kids, let's take your bags up to your rooms."

I almost groan out loud. The last thing I want to see is those stupid rooms. But I can't exactly not follow when Julia yells "Yay! I can't wait!" and starts running past Jack.

Naturally, the kids get immediately engrossed in the crazy amount of toys already sitting in both their rooms. Looks like Beth's been adding since that first Skype tour. Jack leads me up to my room, which at least doesn't seem to have too much added to it. Except for one thing: the laptop on the desk.

I clear my throat. "You got me a computer?"

Jack pats me on the back. "We thought you'd need your own for school, and we wanted to you to be able to stay in touch with your Colorado friends. Of course, there are rules for it: it goes off at ten o'clock every night, no matter what, and homework always happens first. If you have a Facebook account and things like that, make sure your last name isn't on anything. Careful about websites you're on, of course. If you misuse it in any way, we take it back for a while."

I clear my throat, because I have no idea what to say. This is *crazy*. They bought me my own computer? They don't even know me. And I already have *rules* for it? "You got me a computer?" I finally say again.

Jack laughs. "You'll find out that I'm kind of a tech freak— we've got way too many gadgets around here. We'll get you a cell phone eventually too, but we thought we'd wait so you could pick your own out."

Jack starts back down the stairs. "Get comfortable, okay? We'll have dinner in about an hour and a half."

I crash on top of the comforter. Down the tower stairs, I can hear Julia yelling, "Matt! Matt! Come look at this!" I start to get up, to go downstairs and see what Jules's so excited about. But then I start thinking about Julia and that pink room and those dolls. I decide to lie back down again, just for a minute.


"DUSTY!" SOMEONE'S shaking me. Why is someone shaking me? I groggily open my eyes. It's dark outside, and Jack is leaning over me.

51

"Kiddo, we're about to eat dinner. You want to sleep or eat?" Kiddo? No one's ever called me that before. That's what I always call Matt. I try to sit up suddenly, and Jack holds onto my shoulder. "No rush, Dusty. We just didn't want you to skip a meal."

I put my hand on my stomach, trying to remember the last time I ate. Anyway, I want to get downstairs and see Julia and Matt. I can't believe I fell asleep an hour into being at the new house. What if they've needed me?

I get to the kitchen quickly, hoping to save Matt and Julia from an uncomfortable dinner with these strangers, but they're both talking loudly, battling each other for Beth's attention. She's sitting at the head of the table and they're on either side of her. I notice Julia's hair has been brushed and pulled back into a ponytail and that Matt's face is clean. I wince. I've never had a lot of time to pay attention to that kind of stuff with them.

"Dusty!" Beth's face lights up as I walked in. "We were a little worried you were out for the next week. How's fried chicken sound?"

"Dusty, my new doll's name is Linda and the dog Portia likes me!" Julia starts tugging excitedly on my shirt as I sit down.

"Dusty, I got to take Missy running outside and the TV really is huge!" Matt's eyes are wide with excitement. I nod tensely, and suddenly all the food in front of me doesn't seem very appetizing.

I think I see Beth and Jack exchange a glance. "Let's eat, okay, kids?" Jack ruffles Matt's hair and starts piling our plates high with food. Maybe they think we've never eaten before.

At my first bite of mashed potatoes, though, I feel as if I *have* never eaten before. I'm suddenly starving again, because this is delicious. The kids and I eat and eat, and I notice Jack's eyes are twinkling as he watches us, like he's trying very hard not to laugh. I can't blame him. I don't even want to imagine what we look like.

"Did you make this?" Matt asks, rudely grabbing the serving platter for a third helping of chicken. Even Julia, who is usually so polite and neat around food, isn't stopping for air.

Beth nods. "We both did. Jack did the chicken; I did the side dishes." While we finish off most of what is left on the table, Beth begins plotting out our schedule for the next day. "Of course, we really want you guys to start school as soon as possible, but Jack and I thought it might be best if you had a day to adjust to the area. So I thought tomorrow I'd take you shopping, get you some new clothes for school, show you around a little bit. You can start school on Thursday."

School. Wahoo.

"How's that sound?" Beth is still talking. I'm going to have to get used to that. I'm not used to there being so many other adults around, talking all the time, especially at dinner.

The kids start asking questions about clothes and their new school, and I just look steadily around the kitchen, trying to find anything wrong with it. The floor could use a good sweeping, I notice. There's actually a dust bunny in one corner of it. I catch Jack watching me across the table and I bury my gaze in my plate. It's still strange to look at him and see a mirror image of myself. Shouldn't I be the mirror image of my dad or something? But Matt has that covered.

By the time dinner is over, there are almost no leftovers on the table. At home, this would be the point where the kids do their homework and get ready for bed while I do the dishes, so when we're finished eating, they just sort of stand there and stare at me, waiting for directions.

I'm not sure what to do either, so I figure it's best to just do what we've always done. That makes the most sense, right? I've already started clearing our plates away when I realize that Beth and Jack are staring at me too.

Jack clears his throat. "Dusty, you don't have to do that tonight. We'll establish some kind of chore schedule eventually, but for tonight I'll clear the table."

I don't put the dishes down. Dishes are something that have been part of my life forever. I like the routine I have with Matt and Julia after dinner, and I want to keep it.

I turn to Matt and Julia. "You guys go put your pajamas on and get ready for bed, okay? I'll help Jack and Beth with the dishes and then I'll read to you."

Beth and Jack suddenly look uncomfortable. "Actually, Dusty," says Beth, "I was thinking of having the kids help me take the dogs for a walk."

Julia claps her hands. "I'll find the coats!" Matt yells out. I stand there, holding the dishes. *Fine.*

"Sure, no problem," I tell Beth. "I'll just read to them when you get back."

Beth smiles warmly. "Of course," she says. "I got a bunch of books out of the library; I can't wait for us to read with them." She starts toward the door.

Jack's watching me carefully, so I refuse to let my facial expression change.

Still, as I'm rinsing off the serving dishes a few moments later (I figure I can at least keep that part of my routine), I can't stop the phrase *Who invited you?* from dancing over and over inside my head.


THE SUN is bright in the tower room, brighter than I would expect in this gray place. I can tell I'm waking up late in the morning just from how high the sun is in the sky, and I instantly wonder what time it is. The clock on the bureau reads 10:06. After ten o'clock? I throw off the covers. Matt and Jules are usually awake by seven, even on weekends.

I find my bags in a corner of the room and quickly grab some jeans out of my old duffle. I dimly remember that Beth is supposed to take us shopping today. That's probably a good thing, I realize, counting the many holes ripping their way through my poor old pants.

I realize as soon as I get to the living room that, just like last night, I didn't need to bother rushing down the stairs. Julia and Matt are dressed and sitting in front of some kind of stupid PBS TV show. They're eating giant bowls of cereal. Beth is in the corner of the room sipping on a cup of coffee and reading the paper. "Morning, Dusty," she calls. "What would you like for breakfast?"

Before I answer her, I go over and give Matt a quick shove and Julia a hug. I try to ignore the fact that they grin and immediately go back to their TV show. "I'm okay," I say. "I'll just have some juice." I take off to the kitchen before she can try to come fix it for me.

I'm definitely not hitting it off very well with Beth. Our rough ending to last night is still ringing in my head, and I wonder if it's ringing in hers too. Things were fine when the kids first came in from walking the dog; I was finishing up the dishes with Jack and I told them to get their pajamas on. But Beth decided to give them both baths, and when I walked into Julia's room later, the two of them were curled up on either side of Beth with wet hair and fascinated looks aimed at whatever she was reading. Beth stopped and invited me in, with Julia and Matt begging me to come in too, but we all realized pretty quickly that there wasn't a whole lot of room on the bed for me. I left before their second story was done. It was the first time in months Julia hadn't drifted off to sleep while I was reading to her.

Maybe the whole scene is staying with her too, because she follows me into the kitchen. "So, I thought we'd go shopping soon."

"Sure. I could use some new jeans."

Beth smiles and puts her hand on my shoulder. I tense up, but I don't pull away. "Dusty…." Beth starts to say something, but she stops quickly. "Be ready to go in about forty minutes, okay? That'll give you time to shower." She leaves the room.

Julia comes running into the kitchen, holding one of the Barbies that had been on her new bed the day before. "Dusty! Aunt Beth's taking us to get new clothes!"

I try to smile. "I know. It's great, Julia."

She puts out her arms for another hug, so I swing her around the rooms a few times and get a kiss on my cheek. "I like it here, Dusty." She grins as I put her down. "Will Mom and Dad come here soon too?"

You'd think the biggest burdens of my life in Colorado would be the dishes, the cooking, the laundry, that stuff. Nope. It was always wondering when my parents would finally show up to raise my siblings. It was trying to always explain to them where Mom and Dad were, what Mom and Dad were doing, why they were never around. Now, apparently, new parents have shown up. And I still don't know how to explain what happened to the old ones.

"I don't know, Jules," I finally decide to say.

THINGS JUST get worse as the day wears on.

First we go to some little kids' store in a Burlington mall, where Beth pulls every pink outfit off the store racks and hustles Julia into a changing room with them. Then she finds about a hundred things for Matt and sends him into another one.

In all the time I've spent taking care of Matt and Julia, I've never once shopped with them. When Mom's around, she usually finds time to get them some clothes, and there isn't much money for clothes shopping when she isn't there.

Beth keeps glancing over the partition of Julia's changing room, saying, "We'll get stuff for you next, Dusty." I don't really care that much. It doesn't matter to me what the kids at this new school think of me.

The problem is that Julia keeps flouncing out of the dressing room in new outfits, usually pink or purple, shouting to Beth about how great the clothes are. Then she looks at me and says things like, "Dusty, look at my new shirt!" I finally pull a chair up into the corner and try to drown out the fact that Matt and Julia are happier than I've seen them in a long time.

Matt gets sick of trying clothes on long before Julia. He sacks out in a chair next to me, and Beth finally decides it's probably time for lunch.

"Dusty, aren't you hungry?" Beth has ordered Matt and Jules grilled-cheese sandwiches, and I have a bacon cheeseburger in front of me. I can't eat a bite of it, though. We're in probably the nicest restaurant I've ever been in, with fancy waiters and bartenders all around, and the kids are loving every minute of it. I just want to go back to Colorado Springs and eat ramen again for a while. Yup, that would definitely be easier. I shake my head. "Nah, not feeling well. Do we have to go shopping for me today? Can it wait?"

Beth eyes my worn jeans for a moment. "Dusty, I really don't think you can make it through the rest of the week without a decent pair of pants. Give me your sizes and I'll get you some while you're in school tomorrow, okay?"

Matt is instantly concerned. "Dusty, why are you sick?"

He comes around the table to stand next to me, and I grin a little, thinking of how quickly he can become such a serious kid. The look on his face is the same one he wore when Julia first got sick, and I know him well enough to know what he's thinking. I stop smiling. "I'm okay, Matt."

I am and I'm not. I'm not sure if it's watching Matt and Julia moon over Beth's every move, or the fact that I have to start a new school tomorrow, but I'm just not hungry, and I sure don't want to go shopping. This move's turning out to be just excellent for my emotional health, I think, as I remember Race in the hospital cafeteria not that long ago.

When we get back to Jack and Beth's, I head to Julia's room with her and ask her to tell me a story about one of her new Barbies. I figure that way I can try to rest without feeling like I'm abandoning her or whatever.

It has to be late when I feel someone lifting me. "Jack?" I croak.

"Hey, kiddo." He has carried me halfway up the tower stairs already. "You must be one tired kid." He's grinning like the Cheshire Cat in that awful book Mom used to like to read to me sometimes. *Alice in Wonderland? Alice in Neverland?* I think there's a movie, too, but I've never really wanted to see it—that cat terrified me. "Every time you disappear for awhile you fall asleep. Are you feeling any better?"

So much for not abandoning Julia with her brand-new family. "I'm fine," I mumble. It's like my worst nightmare is happening in front of me: I keep disappearing on Matt and Julia, just like our parents always have.

We reach the bedroom before I can get a clear thought in my head and ask Jack to put me down. He plops me onto the bed and starts pulling my shoes off. "I can do that," I say, pushing him away as I sit up. Jack rubs my hair, and I don't even try to stop myself from pulling away.

"Hey, school tomorrow, okay? So get some more sleep. Beth said you looked pretty pale at lunch; you still kind of do."

I don't really answer him; I just pull my shoes off. It's late, and I fell asleep on Julia's new pink bed while she was trying to tell me a story.

# CHAPTER
# FOUR

*ONE YEAR Earlier*

*"Dusty, what's up with you?"*

*Dusty came out of his thoughts, startled, and realized the McDonald's he and Race were sitting in was almost empty. "Where'd everybody go?"*

*"They left. You've been, like, lost in space. You okay?"*

*Dusty shook his head, trying to get the fantasy he'd been in the middle of gone—as soon as possible. "I'm fine. Why wouldn't I be?" He wadded up the cheeseburger wrapper in front of him. "I finally have a night off, right? Mom's home with Matt and Julia, and not even yelling at us right now, and I got to go to the movies with you and the other guys. What would be wrong?"*

*Race's eyes narrowed. "Yeah, that's what I was wondering."*

*Dusty squirmed uncomfortably. The problem was that Daniel Garcia-Allan had come with them, and lately everything about Daniel had been making Dusty nervous.*

*Not that Daniel had been doing anything wrong. Daniel was just being himself—funny, loud, exciting. That night he had almost gotten thrown out of the theater for starting a popcorn fight with Race.*

59

*The problem was that when Daniel did stuff like that, it made Dusty… well, it made him feel the way he was pretty sure girls were supposed to be making him feel. And that was starting to worry him.*

*It was also starting to worry him that he really wanted to run his hands through Daniel's dark-brown hair, and sit next to him in the movie theater, and hang out with him more.*

*Race was still looking at him, and Dusty thought for a second about just blurting the problem out. But how could he? Race would hate him, right? Race would never talk to him again.*

*"Everything's fine, dude. I guess I'm just worried about leaving my mom for too long with Matt and Julia, you know? I mean, she could lose it again anytime. Let's call your mom to come get us, okay?"*

*Race looked like he might argue for a second, but then he pulled out his cell phone and started dialing. Dusty sighed in relief.*

I'M UP early the next morning. Not only because I've now slept more in two days than I slept in the previous month, but also because I know school is coming. I'm already done with my shower and ready to wake up Matt and Julia when Beth comes trotting up the stairs in sweats. She has a dog leash in her hand.

"Wow, Dusty, you're already up! I was coming to pull you guys out of bed. School today!" She is, like, way too chipper. You can tell she's not heading off to her first day at a new school.

"I'll wake the kids up," I announce. "I like doing it."

She hesitates. "Umm… okay," she says slowly. "Why don't you wake up Matt and I'll wake up Julia?"

It's a compromise, but it's better than nothing. I'm all too aware that I'm not going to see them the rest of the day, so I embrace the compromise and wake Matt up with an epic tickling match.

Jack is already eating breakfast when we come down to the kitchen a little later. My stomach growls, and I realize I haven't eaten in almost a day. "Good, Dusty, you look ready!" Jack turns to bring a cereal bowl to the sink. "Can we leave in twenty?"

I nod and pour milk on a huge bowl of cereal. These people sure like to leave in exact amounts of minutes. "Are we dropping the kids off on the way? 'Cause they may need a little longer than that; Matt can take forever to eat breakfast sometimes."

"I do not." Matt shoves me rudely in the back and sticks his tongue out at me.

Jack shakes his head. "Actually, Dusty, we're going in a separate direction, and I've got to be at school a little early, so Beth will drop the little kids off."

Of course. I should've known that was coming.

Matt stands in front of Jack and puts his hands on his hips. "Hey, I'm not little, Uncle Jack!"

Jack mocks terror. "Oh no, he's heard me! The big one has heard me!" He grabs Matt up and lifts him in the air. "What if he gets me, Dustin? What if he gets me?" He swings Matt around a few times, with Matt cracking up the whole way.

"My name's Dusty." I say it loudly as Jack is setting Matt down.

"Huh?"

"My name's Dusty. Nobody calls me Dustin."

Jack doesn't ask me why not, and I'm glad. "Okay. C'mon, Dusty, we'll get going. Meet me in the truck after you eat."

We're at least ten minutes into the trip before either of us says anything. "So, Dusty," Jack begins, concentrating hard on the road, "I arranged for one of my hockey players to show you around the school."

"One of your hockey players?"

Jack glances over. "Yeah, I'm Colby's hockey coach. I've never mentioned that?" I don't answer, so he keeps going. "His name's Emmitt LaPoint; he's a really good kid. He's actually a junior, but his brother Casey's a freshman like you, and I figured you might like them."

I can't see myself being friends with members of the hockey team. I've never played hockey in my life or even seen a game. Prescott doesn't have real sports teams. Everybody there just plays for the Parks and Rec teams. "Does his brother play hockey too?"

Jack shakes his head. "Actually, no. He used to. From what Emmitt told me, he was really talented; his peewee coaches thought he'd be the next Gretzky. But he quit somewhere in junior high. He's really into skateboarding now; he's been really involved with the skateboarding club at Colby."

Suddenly I'm interested. "Colby has a skateboarding club?"

"Sure. You still like skateboarding, Dusty? I thought you weren't into it anymore."

I feel my face burn. Caught. "Well, it's more like I've never had my own skateboard, so I don't know much."

"That's great, Dusty," Jack says enthusiastically, and I'm instantly suspicious. Why does Jack think it's great that I like skateboarding? "I mean, Beth and I were hoping there was an activity you could get into once you moved here." I don't answer him, and we spend the rest of the trip in silence.

A tall kid, who I can only assume is Emmitt, is waiting outside Jack's office when we arrive at Colby. "Hey, Emmitt." Jack puts down his bag to unlock his office and motions for us to shake hands. "Emmitt LaPoint, this is Dusty Porter. Not Dustin. Dusty Porter, this is Emmitt LaPoint. Not Emmy."

He seems to think that's pretty funny, but I'm not amused. Emmitt cracks a little bit of a smile, but he's all business in a matter of seconds. "Nice to meet you, Dusty. You sure look like Coach Morton."

I guess I'm going to be hearing that a lot around this school, considering we're mirror images.

"Hey, Coach, do you know his locker assignment?"

Jack frowns as he finally gets his office door unlocked. He fishes around inside his bag for a moment before he comes up with a green slip of paper. "Here, Dusty. It's the total enrollment package. Locker assignment, homeroom location, schedule."

Emmitt looks over my shoulder at the paper in front of me and nods. "Cool. Okay, Coach, I'll start taking him around the school before everybody gets here."

Maybe I suddenly have a deer-in-the-headlights look, because Jack puts his hand on my shoulder. "Is that okay, Dusty? I mean, if you guys can give me a few minutes, I can come around with you."

Excellent—my uncle baby-sitting me on my first day. "No, Jack, I'll be fine."

A few minutes later, Emmitt and I are walking down the wide school hallway. Emmitt studies locker numbers as he looks for mine, and I study Emmitt. He has dark-blond hair that's kind of curly and hangs down around his ears. His eyes are really green, as green as—well, once I start thinking about it, my dad's. Even though he doesn't look that big, you can tell he's pretty built. Must be the hockey. He's wearing khakis and a button-up shirt. I look down at my black polo and old jeans and wonder what the other kids at Colby are going to be dressed like. The fact is that this guy is really good-looking, and I can't keep my eyes off him as he explains what the classrooms are on each side of the hall we're walking down. I'm definitely going to get lost at some point during the day.

It was probably late last school year—the end of eighth grade—when I got really worried about the fact that I just didn't think girls were all that amazing-looking. Race could babble on about them for hours. *Jasmine has the most amazing boobs, I'd love to get to second base with her* and *Did you see those jeans Erin's wearing today? Holy shit, that ass, Dusty.* Jasmine's boobs and Erin's ass never did anything for me, but when I had my first PE class with Daniel Garcia-Allan, I started to realize why. I got a B in that PE class only because I missed most of the directions Coach Cartwright gave us.

At first it completely freaked me out, and I spent about a month trying to figure out what I was going to do. Then I realized there wasn't much *to* do. I was so busy taking care of Matt and Julia that it wasn't like I had time to date anyway, and Race always just assumed that was why I didn't ask any girls out. I'd still dance with a few of them at Prescott dances, and nobody ever seemed to guess that if I had it my way I would have been dancing with a six-foot-three basketball player who definitely did *not* have C-cups.

Emmitt finds my locker for me, and I tear my eyes away from him long enough to get it open. It isn't too far away from my homeroom—only about two hallways—so mornings will be a breeze.

Emmitt proceeds to lead me on a tour of my schedule, taking me to each of my classes one by one. He's thorough. He hits every detail of the school, which is big, right down to where I am welcome to sit with him and his brother in the cafeteria. He's so thorough that I manage to forget how amazing his eyes are long enough to actually figure out where my classes are.

"So, do you do this as a job or something?" I finally ask him. "You really have a routine."

Emmitt starts laughing. "Nah. I just did this at the beginning of the year for my little brother, so I sort of repeated it for you. I think that's why Coach asked me to do it." By this time we've circled back to my locker, but he hangs around and keeps talking. "Coach is a cool guy, but I didn't think you'd want your uncle showing you around on your first day or anything."

Very true. Since "Wanna go to the movies this weekend?" probably isn't an appropriate question to ask at this point, I decide to ask something else I've been curious about. "Is your brother really into skateboarding or something?" I haven't seen any skate parks around town or any kids with skateboards coming into school, but that doesn't necessarily mean anything. I like to skateboard, and I sure don't carry a board around with me—I don't even own one.

Emmitt rolls his eyes. "Obsessed, for about the last two years. Why, you into boarding too?"

I start unpacking my backpack and loading notebooks into my locker. The notebooks are all empty, white, brand-new and newly purchased by Beth. Already I miss my old history notebook from Prescott, completely covered with the Calvin and Hobbes cartoons I've been drawing on the cover since August. "Yeah, a little. I'd love to find out where there are some skate parks around here."

"Sure, no problem," Emmitt answers. "I'll make sure Casey sits with us during lunch so he can tell you all about that scene. Me, I'm just into hockey."

By now it's almost time for homeroom. The hallways have started to completely fill up, and people are yelling hello to Emmitt from every direction. "Man, I gotta get my stuff," he says. "You gonna find your homeroom okay?"

I look around at the giant crowd of people that seems to have materialized around me. "I'll be okay." I grab my books and start pushing my way through the hall as Emmitt heads in the opposite direction.

I'm not delusional. I'm completely aware—way too aware—that there is almost zero chance he's like me about the girl thing, and that makes me wonder why everything about my life has to be so frigging unfair all the time.


"So, HOW'D it go?" Jack asks me, with great interest, on the ride home.

"Okay. It went just fine."

It really did. All my teachers seem decent; only two even brought up how much Jack and I look alike. Everybody at Colby dresses kind of differently, so my clothes didn't stand out too much or anything. This girl named Alicia started talking to me in French class and made sure I didn't look like a total loser in the two other classes we had together. (I'm a little worried she's developing a crush on me, but I've decided to stress about that later.) Even though the kids at Colby look way different from the kids at my old school—there were lots of black and Hispanic kids at Prescott, while everyone in northern Vermont seems to be white—they act basically the same.

Casey turned out to be really cool. He and Emmitt are a lot alike; they're both really easy to get along with. Of course, they dress nothing like each other. Where Emmitt is sort of preppy, Casey is all skateboarder, and his outfit of the day consisted of skinny jeans, Converse sneakers, and a shirt that said ONLY AN IDIOT WOULD TAKE THE TIME TO READ THIS T-SHIRT. He'd introduced himself to me at lunch by handing me a cheeseburger and launching into a long explanation of why the skate park below the tracks was way better than the one closer to the school. I couldn't even find space to get a word in. When he was finally done, he looked up at me and said, "You wanna join the skate club? We practice together." I didn't get to answer before he started going on about the differences between his two favorite skateboards. He even offered to lend me a skateboard to practice with when I finally got the chance to mention that I didn't have one.

Of course, there had been some jackass in my American history class who'd snorted loudly when the teacher introduced me and made some stupid comment about whether I was as dumb as my twin. I decided not to mention that to Jack. I'd already figured out that the kid was probably some asshole Jack had failed in one of his math classes, and anyway, the teacher had nailed him to the wall and sent him to the office. Why make a big deal out of it?

"Good," says Jack," waking me out of my daze. "I'm glad it went okay. What did you think of Emmitt and Casey?"

I try not to crack a smile thinking about Casey's nonstop speeches at lunch and Emmitt's... well, Emmitt's everything. "They were cool." I suddenly feel like I should say something else. I mean, if it weren't for Jack, I might've had to eat lunch in the corner of the cafeteria by myself. "Uhh... thanks... for introducing me and all." Jack just nods and smiles.

We don't talk much of the rest of the way home. The kids are already home, and Julia greets me at the door by literally flinging herself into my arms. "*Dusty!* School is so much fun! My teacher is really nice and she likes my doll and she let us use markers to color and Aunt Beth is going to be one of the room mothers...."

Jules keeps talking, but I almost drop her when she says that. Beth's going to be a room mother at Danville Elementary?

I'm just setting down Julia, who is still talking a mile a minute, when Matt comes rushing in. "Dusty, I already joined the soccer team! And Aunt Beth's even going to help out the coach!"

I smile faintly and lead the kids into the kitchen with me. Something in the oven smells really good, and I can see a pie on the counter in the back. How does this woman have time for all this?

"Hey, Dusty!" Beth pulls a casserole dish out of the oven and motions me over. "How was your first day of school?"

"Uhh... fine, I guess. You're going to help out at the elementary school?"

"Oh, of course!" Beth dips a spoon into the casserole dish. "I've always volunteered there anyway. My business does really well without all the work it took when I first got it started; I have plenty of time to volunteer.... Dusty, are you feeling any better? You still look a little pale. Are you coming down with something?"

I shake my head. "Of course not. I feel fine. Hey, Beth, could I help out at their school too, you think?"

Beth looks up in surprise. "I don't see why not.... I'll talk to the principal and ask. It's just that you're usually going to be in school during the volunteer hours. But maybe you can help out with Matt's soccer team too."

As in *also,* I think. As in *along with you.* "I have a lot of homework," I say gruffly. "Hey, Matt, Jules, let's go in the living room and I'll help you with your homework."

Jules shakes her head widely, spreading her blond hair quickly around her face. "We already did it! Aunt Beth helped us. Now she's going to let us walk the dogs with her."

I ruffle Jules's hair and try to smile.

I decide to do my homework upstairs; suddenly the kitchen doesn't smell as good as it did a few minutes earlier.

"MR. PORTER—are you ready to share your topic with the class?"

I like Mr. Lewis, all in all, as a history teacher. He's pretty relaxed, and our big project this semester is to choose a topic in American history that interests us and give a presentation on the subject. I generally like school stuff like that, where you get to decide what you want to learn about and sort of go at your own pace with it.

Still, I hate talking in this class. Every time I do, that stupid kid who made that remark about Jack on the first day of school finds some way to say something to me, and a whole group of his friends laugh. Mr. Lewis yells at them for it whenever he notices it, and a lot of the time he sends the jerk, Rick, out of the room, but I'm still not happy when Mr. Lewis asks me to get up in front of everybody—even if everyone in the class has to present their topic today.

I mean, I've only been in this school a week, and I'm already coming to the conclusion that I'm going to have to do something about this Rick guy pretty quickly.

Not that I have a lot of options in that area. Rick is about five inches taller and sixty pounds heavier than me.

I get up slowly to go the front of the room, and I instantly hear snickers behind me.

"Um, I'm going to do my presentation on the Pike Expedition. The Pike Expedition began in 1806—"

"Excuse me, excuse me, sir!"

I do my best not to roll my eyes as Rick starts yelling out from the back of the classroom. Mr. Lewis sighs heavily and asks, "Rick, could you try raising a hand sometime?"

"Sir, I'm thinking there's no way you can grade this presentation fairly. His uncle is probably gonna make sure he gets an A no matter what he says."

I hear some of Rick's cronies laugh, but Mr. Lewis just dryly says, "An assistance you could certainly use, Mr. Snyder. Detention."

Rick mumbles about how unfair that is, and I finish my presentation, pulling my desk chair out a little harshly once I get back to my seat. I'm definitely going to have to figure out what this dude's problem is.

After class Mr. Lewis asks to speak with me, and it doesn't take Miss Marple to figure out what he wants to talk about. It's going to make me late for lunch, but I pull up a chair next to his desk anyway. He's a decent guy, and I knew there was no way he was going to let this whole Rick thing go.

Mr. Lewis doesn't beat around the bush. "Have you told your uncle about the hard time Rick Snyder's been giving you since you got here?"

I shake my head. "No… it's not a big deal. I can handle him. I mean, it seems like he's just pissed off at Jack or something."

Mr. Lewis kind of half-smiles. "How true. Rick was the star of our hockey team. Your uncle was forced to remove him because… well, let's just say Rick wasn't a very stable player." I snort. That's got to be an understatement. "Rick's been harboring quite the grudge ever since. I've almost said something to Jack myself, but I rather had the impression you wouldn't be the type to appreciate that. Would I be correct in that assumption?"

Hell, yes. Not only would that be letting Rick win, but it would also be letting Jack know that I need him somehow. "I'd appreciate it if you didn't say anything, Mr. Lewis. I mean, I'm glad you send Rick out when he's wrecking class and all, but other than that, I'd like to handle this myself."

Maybe it's my imagination, but I think Mr. Lewis looks impressed. "All right. If you're sure. Just don't forget that your uncle and I are both here for you anytime you decide you need us, all right?" I nod, and he goes back to talking. "So, Zebulon Pike, eh? That's an interesting topic. I don't think anyone else will be choosing it."

"Yeah, well…." I shrug. "I'm from Colorado Springs."

His eyes light up. "Ah, home of Pikes Peak! I see. Do you mind if I ask why you chose Zebulon? There are far so many aspects of Colorado Springs history you might have chosen."

I'm pretty good at shrugging when I'm talking to teachers, so I keep with what works and do it again. "I dunno. We were just starting to learn about him in school before I moved. I thought it was kind of interesting that he got the mountain named after him even though he didn't finish climbing it."

"Yes... do you find it to be of great importance that he didn't make it to the top?"

Of course I don't really know the answer to that, which is why I'm researching Zeb Pike. "I don't know much about him yet. I mean, that's sort of what I wanted to find out—whether or not it mattered if he got to the top. And if he really wanted to turn back, or wanted to die trying, or whatever, and how he still ended up getting the mountain named for him. 'Cause, shouldn't it have been named after the Native Americans who lived there first anyway?" I throw that on at the end partly in homage to Ms. Carlson and partly because it really does sound right.

Mr. Lewis just smiles. "I look forward to seeing what you learn in your research, Dusty," he says.


I ASK Casey for more info about Rick at lunch. He is knee-deep in a Sloppy Joe, making a good case for why it's called that. His face is covered in meat and sauce.

"Rick Snyder? He's giving you trouble?"

"Sort of." I tell him about history class, and Casey snarls. "Just like that moron to be in a freshman class his junior year. He's got no brain cells, I swear. Drank 'em all away." He chugs his milk and finally wipes some of the meat off his face, which at least makes it easier to take him seriously. "Anyway, Dusty, that's why he hates your uncle so bad. He was the star of the team last year, but Coach Morton kicked him off during the season for drinking and some other stuff, too, I think. Emmitt was thrilled—he was the only star left."

That does explain a lot.

At least, other than Rick, school is okay. It's school. It's routine. Essays, notes, grades, books—a part of life I've always handled just fine. It's all the other stuff I still seem to be having problems with.

Beth is a happy room mother at Danville Elementary, and Matt's joined the soccer team. Every morning I say good-bye to the kids and wait as long as possible before Jack pulls me out of the house and away from them. When school is over, I wait impatiently for Jack to be done with meetings and other teacher stuff. We head home, and I hope all the way to make it there before the kids finish their homework, but they're always done and playing by the time we make it to the house. We have dinner, and if Beth hasn't manage to usurp all the bedtime duties while I frantically do *my* homework, sometimes I get to read Matt and Julia a story before bed.

Then there's the Emmitt... thing. I don't feel like I can really call it a problem, because it isn't. It isn't anything. Casey and I are spending more and more time together at lunch and in between classes, and we usually eat or hang out with Emmitt. The more we do, the more I want to spend time with this guy. Everything I learn about him just makes me like him even more. He's incredibly smart—currently fourth in his class, but he is pretty sure he'll lock in third by the end of the year. He's the starting forward on the school's hockey team, which almost made it to the state championship last year. (Apparently Jack is a pretty good coach.) He's as serious about some things as he was about being my tour guide, but he can also be really funny and relaxed. At lunch he once snorted milk up his nose because he was laughing so hard over a movie he and Casey saw that weekend.

What am I supposed to do? Ask the starting forward of the Colby hockey team, who appears to be about as straight as a 180 degree line (that's right, I can pay attention in Geometry) to have dinner? One thing's clear: I'm either going to have to learn to like girls or look forward to a life of solitude. At least Alicia can't get enough of me. Last week I had to tell her to tone down the Facebook messages because I don't have time to answer them all.

I desperately need a break from both issues, so I can't help but really look forward to the upcoming weekend, when Matt has his first big Danville soccer game.


IT'S THE Friday morning before that game, and it seems like my break is finally in sight. Jack's driving us to school when he puts his hand on my forehead for a second. "What?" I demand, looking at him warily. I have been working so hard to be okay with Beth and Jack taking over Matt and Julia's life, and I think I've been doing a pretty good job. What does Jack want now?

Jack looks over at me out of the corner of his eye. "Oh, nothing. You've just been so quiet lately, and Beth thinks you fall asleep too easily. She wants me to take you to the doctor."

Screw that. I'm fine and I know it. I only fall asleep when I don't want to be awake anymore. "I'm great, Jack. Just tired from school, I guess."

Jack clears his throat quietly. "Dusty," he says, "have you given any more thought to seeing a counselor?"

Not this again. When Matt and Jules and I first got to Vermont, Jack and Beth made a lot of noise about getting us a shrink to help us deal with "everything we'd gone through." Matt and Julia ended up seeing their school counselor regularly, but I told Jack and Beth I didn't want anything to do with a therapist. I thought they'd let it go—apparently not. "Jack, I told you before, I don't want a shrink, okay? I'm just tired."

Jack looks like he wants to argue with me about that but seems to stop himself. It's a few minutes before he says anything else. "Well, listen. I've got a staff meeting after school today, and I know for a fact it's going to go for a while. How about seeing if Emmitt and Casey want to hang out after school? They live nearby."

I perk up so quickly my own smile surprises me. That's a great idea. Casey has been asking me when he can take me to the skate parks in the area, and I'm willing to bet he'll still lend me a skateboard. Not to mention that Emmitt will most likely come with us. He and Casey are almost as close as Matt and I are—maybe closer. They spend an awful lot of time together, especially for brothers who are so completely different.

"Sure, Jack. I'll ask 'em." Whaddya know, for once I'm not going to be in any hurry to rush Jack home and take the kids' evening time away from Beth.

Casey's reaction at lunch is impressive. "Right *on!*" he exclaims loudly through a mouth of french fries. "Luckily for you, I just happen to keep an extra skateboard in Emmitt's truck. I'll show you the park below the tracks I've been talkin' about. So, I've gotta show you this new ramp they just put in...." I have to admit, it's cool hanging out with Casey. Aside from giving me lots of access to Emmitt, the fact that he's friends with, or somehow knows, almost everyone in the ninth grade means that I don't get hassled by any of the crowds within the school except Rick's. Casey is just one of those naturally cool guys who doesn't have to be anything but himself. He's just so relaxed—like Race.

Race. I haven't thought about him much since I arrived in Vermont. I'm not about to start now, when I am finally going to get to skateboard with somebody who probably won't throw me under a bus if I ever need help.

It's starting to get really cold in the afternoons, so I grab my heavy coat the second the final school bell rings. Casey and Emmitt are already waiting for me on the front steps when I get there.

"Jeez." Emmitt shivers. "It's freezing out here. You guys really wanna skateboard?"

Casey flips his board up in the air. "Dude, no air touches me when I skate. You know that."

Emmitt rolls his eyes. "Dusty, sometimes I'm amazed his head even fits through doors."

Casey rolls his eyes back and shoves his brother, and we start the short walk to Emmitt's truck.

Casey squeezes me in between him and Emmitt in the truck's small cab, and all I can do is hope that nothing about my reaction to being this close to Emmitt will give me away. I must hide my emotions even better than I think I do, because neither brother says anything out of the ordinary on the way to the park. When we finally pull up, I wonder what Emmitt will do while Casey and I skateboard—he seems to think skateboarding is pretty stupid. Then he pulls a pair of rollerblades out of the back of the truck, along with an extra skateboard for me. I realize how serious about hockey this guy must be.

Emmitt laces up his blades and starts doing some pretty impressive moves around the perimeter of the park—he's going backward, looping, making other moves that probably have names I could never even imagine. He's a natural at it; it's like his feet were meant to exist on blades. I'm having trouble looking away from him, and it takes Casey's loud babbling to finally remind me that I'm supposed to be here to skateboard, not ogle his brother.

Casey immediately starts inspecting how I stand on my board. "Pretty good… you know your stuff." He hikes up his pants and grabs his board. "Follow what I do…. I'm going to teach you the difference between regular and goofy position."

That's pretty easy—I've always known those; I've just never known what they're called—but then Casey starts going into ollies. "C'mon, Dust!" He's an accomplished coach. "Bend your knees and brace for the impact before you go down." He goes over everything he thinks I need to know, from good position to the best facial expression to have when you hit the ground.

Eventually the wind starts to pick up, and Casey stops telling me how to hold my hips long enough to notice that Jack's meeting should be done soon. He gestures to Emmitt, who skates over to us effortlessly.

"Dusty, what are you doing for Halloween?" Emmitt moves to put his shoes back on, and Casey's eyes light up. "Oh yeah! I can't believe I almost forgot to tell you about Aaron's party."

"Party?" I can't remember going to a *real* party—something that wasn't for a birthday or run by parents—well, ever. There were always more important things to do. "What kind of party?"

"Dude, it's gonna be awesome…. Aaron is on the hockey team with Emmitt. His mom is going out of town that night and he's gonna have a party. Emmitt hasn't decided if he's going to let me go with him yet, but I think he will." He tosses me a KitKat bar from his jacket pocket. "Now I know for sure he's going to, if he's inviting you."

Emmitt shrugs. "You didn't realize you already wore me down? You may as well start inviting all the other little freshmen. If we're going to let you guys in, we're at least going to do this right and use it as an opportunity to prove how much better the junior class is."

He and Casey walk back to the truck, arguing about whether or not more freshman or juniors will show up to the party and which class is really superior. I trail behind. Every memory I have of Halloween involves taking the kids trick-or-treating. There's no way I can disappear on them for their first Halloween in Vermont. There's no way I *want* to, I remind myself, thinking suddenly of Beth.

Emmitt laughs at something Casey has said, and he winks at me as he climbs into the truck. "You better come, Dusty," he tells me. "I always need everyone I can to keep an eye on Casey here."

It's the wink that always gets me. Why does he have to wink?

# CHAPTER FIVE

*THREE YEARS Earlier*

*"What are you going to do if she's still not home?"*

*Race whispered the question to Dusty because he was holding Julia's hand, and Dusty had made it very clear he didn't want to worry Matt and Julia about the fact that their Mom hadn't come home yet. "I don't know. Nothing, I guess. I mean, she's been gone for five days so far and we're doing okay."*

*Race didn't think Dusty was doing very okay. He had dark circles around his eyes, and he'd fallen asleep during math that day. Dusty had told the teacher his mom wasn't feeling well and he'd had to stay up to help take care of her.*

*Race wanted to tell Dusty he needed to say something to his mom about what was going on. He was pretty sure his mom would know what to do. He was not about to suggest that again, though. He had mentioned that yesterday morning and Dusty just about bit his head off. Dusty was his best friend, but he had a temper sometimes, and Race didn't want to upset him anymore than he already was.*

*He couldn't imagine what he would do if his mother just left for days without even telling him. Of course, Dusty's mother had been gone before, so maybe Dusty was used to it now. She had never left for more than a night, though, and Race knew the fact that she wasn't home yet had to be making Dusty really nervous.*

*They arrived at the door of the apartment, Race still holding Julia's hand and Matt at Dusty's side. Dusty took a deep breath and opened the apartment door.*

*And the smell of brownies immediately filled the air.*

*"Mom?" Dusty walked into the kitchen, inhaling the scent. Race followed.*

*"Dusty, baby!" Their mother threw up her hands and hugged each one of her kids. Race watched, amazed at how happy she looked to see them. Sometimes she was so mean to Dusty. "I've missed you! I knew you'd take great care of Matthew and Jules, though."*

*Dusty just nodded, looking dazed.*

*"I wanted to make you brownies to thank you." She picked up Julia and kissed Matt's hair. "Did you miss me, babies? I missed you."*

*"Yeah!" Julia buried her own head in her mother's shoulder. "Mama, I missed you lots!"*

*Matt nodded. "Me too, Mama."*

*She carried Julia into the other room, Matt beside her, telling them about a present she'd brought them.*

*Race cleared his throat. "Why didn't you at least ask her where she's been?"*

*Dusty shrugged and started cutting into the brownies. "I didn't think it really mattered."*

"GO, MATT, go!"

I can't figure out who's louder, Jack or me. We're sitting together on the bottom row of the bleachers at the Danville third and fourth grade soccer game. Beth is out on the field helping the team, right where I want to be, so I've decided I'm just going to be the loudest person in the cheering section instead. I've forgotten, though, that Jack coaches hockey. He has a pretty impressive vocal range.

Matt is the new star of the team, you can tell. They pass him the ball at least 50 percent of the time, and he has already scored two of Danville's three goals. The other team hasn't even come close to scoring yet, and you can tell they're already beat. It's pretty awesome to watch. Julia clings to my hand, asking "Who's winning, Dusty, who's winning?" every three minutes or so.

Overall, it's a great time. If I didn't have to watch Beth on the field, handing water bottles to kids and constantly patting Matt's shoulder, it would be an all-time great day.

Matt comes straight up to me the second the final whistle blows. "We won, we won!" he shouts.

I swing him up in a bear hug. "I know! Great job!"

Beth comes running behind him. She's wearing a tracksuit composed of Danville's colors—green and white—and she looks like one the most dedicated parents there. I kind of hope she's freezing in the tracksuit.

Beth grabs up Julia from where she sits next to me. "Did you see that, Jules? Your brother scored two goals!"

I stop cheering with Matt for a moment to stare her right in the eye. Did she just call my sister *Jules*?

I want to make sure I don't wreck Matt's victory celebration in any way, so I wait to say anything until after we've gone out to eat and are back at the house. Jack settles down in the living room and asks if we want to watch a movie. Matt and Julia cheer and join him, but Beth says she has some work to do out in her real estate office. I don't debate whether or not to say something to her for very long. Pretty soon I'm heading out to the shed.

The walk to the shed building is dark and frigid; it wasn't that warm to begin with today, and it feels like it's dropped another ten degrees since Matt's game. I open the door to the office and call out for Beth. I've never been out here to her office before. I have no idea what she really even does out here—I just know she sells houses.

"Dusty?" Beth smiles as she comes around the corner and sees me. "Hey! What are you doing here?"

I shuffle my feet uncomfortably for a while before I say anything. "I sorta need to talk to you," I mumble.

Beth smiles even more widely, and I'm pretty sure she thinks that it's a good thing I've come out to see her. Somehow, I don't care enough to stop, though. "C'mon inside," she says. "See what my office looks like."

I stay where I am, on the edge of the doorway, in the dark interior of the hall. The hallway is lined with real estate certificates and framed photos of houses and property. Past the hallway I can see papers and file folders strewn about a large oak desk. I can see it just fine from here, I think. "Nah.... I'll just stay here. This won't take very long. Uhh… listen, Beth, I'd kinda prefer if you didn't call Julia 'Jules' anymore."

Surprise writes its way across Beth's face. "Dusty, I'm afraid I don't understand… why?"

Something inside me is untwisting itself slowly, but I don't feel a thing. All I hear is the air rushing by my head, and all I see is a blank face in front of me. "I guess, I mean...." I know I'm mumbling, but so what? "That was Mom's old nickname for Julia, and only Matt and I really ever call her that." That's a lie; Race called her that all the time, but it's not like any of the rest of this makes sense anyway. That *was* Mom's nickname, and I kind of can't stand her most of the time, so why does it bother me that Beth wants to use it?

Beth's facial expression has slowly gone from one of surprise to distress as I speak. "Dusty…. I really don't understand this. You don't consider Jack and me part of your family? Is that the problem?"

The problem is that I can't explain what the problem is. The problem is that I haven't done homework with Julia or Matt in weeks, and Beth is a room mother at their school, and my own mother, who gave Julia that nickname, didn't even bother to come back home after her daughter had major surgery. And the problem is that sometimes I really like having extra time to hang out with Casey and Emmitt after school. That seems to sum up the *problem*. But I can't say any of that, not without sounding like a crazy person. So I just say, "No, not really."

Beth's face is white, so I turn and let myself out the door.

Outside, I stand for a long moment between the office door and the back door to the house. The sky, as usual, is turning yet another dark gray. The fields stretching out behind me are that same straw-colored brown they were the day we arrived, and everything in my sight looks bleak and hopeless. All those great colorful leaves that had at least been there when we arrived have now fallen off the trees and turned brown. Even the once bright-red house seems dark, a maroon color that looks even angrier than the rest of the landscape. I actually stop for a moment to flip off the hills in front of me— stupid miniature versions of the real mountains back home in Colorado.

I turn and run through the fields, making it almost ten yards from the office before I vomit into the grass.

DINNER IS strange. I don't say much except to Matt and Julia, and Beth and I can't seem to look each other in the eye. Jack, on the other hand, is cheerful and talkative, so I assume Beth hasn't said anything to him about our encounter earlier in the evening. "So, gang," Jack says, stuffing extra green beans into his mouth. "Halloween's coming up… it's this week. What's everyone going as?"

Of course, Jules and Matt still love Halloween. Thankfully, I'm finally past that age where I can really remember the excitement of dressing up as someone else and gathering candy from every direction, but Jack's announcement definitely brings a smile to my face when I think about Emmitt's party invitation.

Julia bangs her fork excitedly on her plate. "I wanna be a princess! I wanna be a princess!"

Matt turns quickly on his chair. "You can't be a princess! My friend Laney is a princess!"

Julia's lips quiver. "I can so be a princess if I want to."

Matt shakes his head hard. "Nuh-uh, it's a rule. Two people can't be the same thing."

I hang onto every word they're saying, astonished. I've never heard them argue like this. Back in Colorado they might have had a tiny disagreement here and there, but Matt has never made Julia look like she's going to cry, I'm sure of that.

I try to force my mouth open, to make them stop, but Jack beats me to it as he passes out more mashed potatoes.

"Matt, there's no reason Julia can't be the same thing as your friend. I'm sure their costumes will be different anyway."

"That's right," Beth suddenly speaks up. "I'll help make both of yours so they'll be different from everybody else's. We'll have to go shopping for costume materials this week." Julia claps her hands together, and I swear I see Beth look at me out of the corner of her eye.

I suddenly feel, for some reason, like I am being challenged to a battle. Maybe Beth is just checking to see where I stand with what she just said, but I take it as a confrontation, a direct affront after our earlier conversation in her office. I clear my throat. "I want to take them trick-or-treating," I demand.

Just to be clear, I'm not even sure where this comes from. Only minutes ago I was daydreaming about that party, and just a day ago I was thinking about how I've never gone to a party like that before. But Matt starts cheering, and Julia says, "Yay! Just like last Halloween," and that seals it for me. After all, what am I going to do at Aaron's party? Drool? Watch Emmitt make out with a bunch of female hockey fans?

Jack glances at me oddly. Beth, I notice, isn't looking at me at all. She gets up to clear her plate. "That's fine, Dusty," she replies. "But just so you know, the houses are too far apart to walk between easily. Jack or I will probably have to drive you guys." She's right, of course. Houses here are a mile apart; it isn't like central Colorado Springs where the kids and I could just walk from place to place.

Somehow, though, the only part of that sentence I hear is "I will probably have to drive you guys," and I'm on my feet in seconds. The shoe has dropped, the sword has fallen, and all that other cliché stuff—it's like I'm Zeb Pike and I've decided I am going to finish climbing this stupid mountain, no matter how much damn snow is in the way.

"Can't you let me have any time with them?" I shout to her back, and she slowly turns from the sink. She looks tired, but so am I, and I keep going. "You bring them to school, you bring them home, you tuck them in, and I never get to see them at all. Can't I have Halloween? All I want is freakin' Halloween! I'm sick of this!" I finish by slamming my water glass down on the table.

But the *most* cliché thing about this little display of temper is that no one's more surprised by this little tirade than me. Not to mention that while I'm yelling at Beth, there's a weird moment when I flash back to the doorway of the apartment of Sunny's and imagine myself yelling at my father like this. A psychologist's dream, that's me.

Jack's face suggests he's just as surprised by this episode as I am. Only Beth seems prepared with a response. "Dusty," she says calmly, clutching a coffee mug tightly, "I understand that you're upset, and we can definitely talk about Halloween, but why don't we go talk in the study?" She glances quickly over at Matt and Julia, who are both staring at me and Beth alternately, eyes wide. Great. I really can't do anything right with them anymore.

Which is probably why I end up just going for broke. "I hate it here!" I explode. "I want to take them back to the Springs! We'll be fine; we were always fine before!"

Beth is about to say something, but Jack stands up. "Dusty," he begins, and I feel the "teacher" tone take over his voice. It isn't really angry, just demanding and powerful. "Go up to your room. I'll be up to talk to you in a minute."

Too bad. "Go to your room" isn't really going to cut it with me right now. "You think I have to listen to you?" I snarl. "I've been on my own a long time, and I don't have to answer to anybody."

Jack cocks an eyebrow at me. "You live in my house. Go."

I reach for Julia and Matt. "C'mon, guys, I'll read you a story." They both start to follow me, still wide-eyed, but Jack shakes his head hard and they stop.

"No, Dusty. We're going to talk, just the two of us." He's still using teacher voice, but he somehow makes it a little gentler when he says to Matt and Julia, "Go on into the living room and play for awhile, okay, guys? Or you can watch TV. I need to talk to your brother."

They make their way out of the room, and I'm left with Beth and Jack staring at me. "Dusty, what's going on?" Jack asks.

The room spins. I watch it go around. It's holding all the things about my life that I just can't seem to conquer. Dad in the doorway of Sunny's. Matt in soccer games I'm not there for. Matt in soccer games I always have to be there for. Beth reading stories to Matt and Julia every night, whether I want her to or not. Race in the dingy cafeteria of an old hospital. Emmitt leaning against my locker before first period. "I hate it here," I half-whisper. In a rush, I run for the door, quickly grabbing my jacket and slamming out of the house.

The cold air hits me hard, and I suddenly feel all of what has just happened. I don't get very far down the road before I hear Jack's truck roaring up behind me. I don't care as much as I should; it really is freezing outside and I have no idea where I'm going anyway. I hear a door slam and Jack walking up to me, but I keep up my quick pace.

Jack catches up with me and grabs me by the shoulder. "Get in the truck, Dusty," he says, sighing. I don't have any more determination to argue. What else am I going to do, freeze to death?

In the truck, Jack waits a few minutes before he says anything. "Dusty, what's really going on here?" he finally asks. "Are you really that upset that Beth's been spending time with Matt and Julia?"

I don't answer.

83

Jack pulls into the driveway and cuts the engine, but he puts a hand on my shoulder to keep me from going anywhere. I stare out the window so that I don't have to look at him. "Listen, Dusty, I know this has been a huge change, and neither Beth nor I expect you to be fine with everything's that happened." He squeezes my shoulder a little, probably wanting me to turn around and look at him. I don't. "Dusty, if you'll just talk to us, we can make this easier on you. If you want to spend more time with Matt and Julia, we can make that happen. I thought you were enjoying spending time with the LaPoints after school."

Oh, if only he knew.

"Dusty, can you do that? Can you try to talk to us about what you're thinking, so that you don't end up screaming at us in the kitchen over trick-or-treating?"

He just doesn't get it, and no matter how much he wants me to, I can't explain it to him. I suddenly start shivering violently. "Whatever," I mumble.

Jack sighs and takes his hand off my shoulder. "Dusty," he says softly, "Beth and I really want to make this work. For all three of you."

I didn't know what I want to make work anymore. So I just go straight to bed. It seems easier that way.

IT'S AMAZING I learn anything at school the next week, because I spend most of it listening to Casey ramble on and on about the plans for Aaron's Halloween party. All I hear is, "Dude, Emmitt says if we drink we have to spend the night, but I think that's an okay idea, don't you? Not too corny?" or "Emmitt says I can't invite too many more people or it will piss Aaron off, but the Spanish club isn't too many more people, right? I mean, there's only like ten of them," and "Man, what do you think about music choices? Aaron says we need more stuff people can shuffle too, but I kind of suck at shuffling." He's so busy helping to make sure this is the "party of the year" that it's Thursday, the day before Halloween, before he remembers to ask if I'm even going.

"So, you coming?" Casey asks me, juggling the piles in his locker before fourth period. I'm waiting for him to get his books for class, and despite how much I've had to listen to about the planning of this party, I'm not planning on going.

"I dunno, dude.... I may take the kids trick-or-treating that night."

Casey looks at me in disbelief. "And miss the fiesta? Anyway, Dusty, don't you need to be able to drive to take them trick-or-treating out in the sticks where you live?"

That stings momentarily, but I try to let it go. "Ah, who knows. We'll see."

Casey is outraged. "Dude, you gotta go! Emmitt and I hang out with you like, all the time now! He was going to introduce you to all his 'hockey' friends." Casey actually uses air quotes for the word *hockey,* as though he's not sure it's a real thing. "Plus, I got Alicia to come! Just for you!"

It takes a lot for me not to roll my eyes. Here we go; it's like the Race thing all over again. I am *definitely* going to have to learn to start liking girls. There has to be some kind of self-help book out there for this kind of problem, right? Put out by James Dobson or somebody?

"I don't know... we'll see. Who else is going?" Casey rattles off a who's-who list of Colby High students. A lot of them are hockey players, as promised, and I wonder if Jack would even say yes if I asked him about the party. I think he might. He really trusts and likes Emmitt, and he doesn't have to know Aaron's parents aren't going to be there.

I'm not sure I can ask him, though. I've barely spoken to him since the night of Matt's soccer game. The drives to and from school are these long uncomfortable loads of silence, with Jack trying to get me to talk about schoolwork and skateboarding and me shrugging at him a whole lot. I kind of know I'm acting like an ass, but I don't really know how to be any different. I don't want to talk to him

85

about school or skateboarding or how I feel about Beth and him spending time with Matt and Julia. I just don't want to talk to him about anything.

Dinners are pretty weird too. Luckily, Matt and Julia talk enough to make up for me not saying anything. They've pretty much proven that television must be ruining kids' attention spans or something, because it's like they've already forgotten about my fight with Jack and Beth. Plus, they have enough Halloween conversation in them to keep us all going for hours. Jules is going to be a princess; Matt has his alien costume. They like to give us all long explanations of the different costumes their friends will be wearing and why some are better than others.

Friday the 31$^{st}$ (zero hour, as Casey has taken to calling it) finds me standing by my locker, telling Casey that I don't think I'm going to make the party that night—apologies and all that. Emmitt comes up to join the conversation and jabs me in the arm. "Why not, Dusty? Is it 'cause you live out in the boondocks? I'll come pick you up, and you can spend the night at Aaron's with us. Coach'll be fine with it. C'mon, we really want you there."

He's killing me, and he doesn't even know it. He just shakes his hair out of his eyes and winks at me, and he could probably get me to rob a bank with him. Still, I stay strong by reminding myself how excited Matt and Julia were about the idea of me trick-or-treating with them. Not to mention that I've hardly seen them all week. Not to mention that Emmitt has most of the girls in school lining up for his number. Not to mention that I am definitely *not* a girl.

I shrug. "Thanks for the offer. If I change my mind, I'll text you, okay?" I avoid their groans by claiming I have to go meet Jack for my ride home, thinking that it's kind of nice to have people so upset that I'm not going to be hanging out with them.

Jack and I are barely through the door that afternoon when Matt and Julia accost us both at the doorway. "Look at my costume! Look!" Julia shrieks, spinning around and around. She does look

86

really cute. She has on some kind of pink princess costume, complete with wand and crown.

Matt's costume is a bright green stereotypical alien figure. He keeps stalking around the room shouting, "Take me to your leader!"

Beth comes into the kitchen with her purse on her shoulder. She kisses Jack hello and gives me a huge smile. "So, I thought we'd leave soon to go trick-or-treating. Are you guys ready?"

Matt and Julia have made my decision for me. They come first; they always have. Plus, if I don't go, it's like I'm letting Beth and Jack win somehow.... I'm not sure why, but I'm pretty sure that's how the whole thing will feel in my head.

I'm just about to answer when Jack, who is pulling his camera out from some cabinet, says, "C'mon, Dusty. I'll come too. We'll make it a big family night."

I stop. Everything stops. Even Matt and Jules seem to sense that something has just changed. Jack looks up from where he is kneeling, his eyes wide. I can practically read his thoughts: *I'm not sorry I said it, but how's he gonna react?*

I'm somewhat proud to say that I don't lash out. I don't lose control, even though I want to.

There's no way I'm going trick-or-treating now, though. This isn't my family. I'm not sure what my family is anymore, but I'm pretty sure this isn't it.

I clear my throat. "Actually, I'm really tired. Long day at school. I kind of just want to take a nap. Is that okay?"

"No, Dusty!" Julia grabs my hand. "We want you to come with us!"

"Yeah, Dusty, yeah!" Matt shoves at me.

They just can't get it. Can't get that I'd never shared them before, and that these aren't the adults I've spend years waiting to share them with.

I ignore any looks Jack and Beth are sharing and hug both Matt and Julia good-bye. "C'mon, guys, you're going to have a great time. I'll go with you next year, I promise."

Matt groans as I head toward the stairs and I almost cave, but one look at Beth keeps me going. I take the stairs to my bedroom two at a time, and I pace in my room, waiting, until I am sure I've heard the last of the kids' excited shrieks. The door slams, a car roars to life, and the sound of gravel lifting off the driveway fills the night.

I grab the cell phone Jack bought me a week or so earlier out of my backpack and quickly text Emmitt. *Can u come pick me up?*

# CHAPTER
# SIX

*SIX MONTHS Earlier*

*Daniel was talking, and Dusty was hanging on every word.*

*"I think it's going to be a great movie. I mean, I know sequels suck sometimes, but Transformers won't be like that. Want to go this weekend?"*

*They were sitting outside the steps of Prescott, watching Matt and Julia and Daniel's brother Chris and a bunch of other elementary kids use the playground. Dusty was wishing that Daniel was a girl, because then this might be a date or something.*

*Instead of Daniel just wanting to hang out with a friend.*

*Then again, Dusty thought, it would probably just be easier to wish that he liked girls the way he was supposed to.*

*"Uhh.... I'd like to. I don't know if I can."*

*"Why not, man? You said you loved the first movie."*

*He had said that—partly because he had and partly because Daniel had said he loved the first movie. "My mom's gone Saturday night. I gotta watch Matt and Jules."*

*"Maybe Sunday afternoon then?"*

*Dusty took in a deep breath. His mom had been gone for over a week. He had no idea if she'd be back by that weekend, but he doubted it.*

*"Let me ask her and get back to you."*

*Daniel shrugged. "Sure, no big deal. What did you think about how they did the special effects, anyway? I sort of thought that...."*

*Dusty tried not to stare while he talked.*

*But he was pretty sure he wasn't succeeding.*

"MAN, CASEY was so excited you changed your mind."

Emmitt's picked me up alone, because apparently Casey was already having too much fun at the party to leave. I try not to twitch at that sentence. *What about you, Emmitt? Were you excited I changed my mind?*

"It's great the way you guys have become such good friends so quickly. It's really good for him."

*That* gets me to turn my head quickly toward Emmitt. Casey is one of the cooler guys in school—friends with everybody, never hurting for company. How the hell is my loser-ass friendship any kind of benefit for him?

I must look incredulous, because Emmitt nods. "I know, he seems, like, superhuman and all that at times. But haven't you noticed that he doesn't really have any close friends?"

I try to come up with someone else Casey talks to as much as he talks to me, and I realize I can't.

"He just… he really doesn't trust people the way he used to before our dad left. He even stopped hanging out with all his elementary and middle school friends the same way after that happened. Mostly because they were all into hockey and he quit when Dad took off, but still…. I got really worried that he was going to keep everyone except me at arm's length for the rest of his life."

It's so strange to hear Emmitt talking about Casey like this. It's true; I do tend to think of Casey as being superhuman. I had no idea their dad had taken off too. Maybe in some weird, subconscious way we get each other because of that. I don't really know what to say, so I decide to go with, "Oh, Casey did play hockey. Jack mentioned that, but Casey never talks about it."

Emmitt laughs. "Yeah, he did. He was a total skating prodigy, actually." He shrugs. "It actually took years for me to get as good as I am now. Casey just stepped on skates and knew what to do. Our dad was so freakin' happy." He looks off into the distance of the long road in front of us, and I start to realize that maybe Emmitt isn't all that superhuman either.

"Your dad was a hockey player too?" I venture. I don't want to ask any really stupid questions, but I don't feel like this is too out of line, and it feels good to be having such a personal conversation with Emmitt. Up until this point, we've never talked about anything more meaningful than tacos versus enchiladas.

Emmitt snorts. "Not exactly. He was just an athlete, and he really wanted his kids to be too. Luckily for him, Casey has always been good at everything athletic, even gymnastics."

"Gymnastics?" I nearly choke. It seems impossible to imagine Casey doing a cartwheel.

"Oh, he never told you about that?" Emmitt laughs hysterically. "It was when he was six. Mom said that if Dad was going to have Case doing all these different sports, she got to pick one too." He nods appreciatively. "And he was great at that too. But in the end, he liked hockey best."

"Uh, Emmitt...." Now I'm definitely going into uncharted territory. "Where is your dad?"

Emmitt concentrates hard on making a left-hand turn into Colby. "Uh, Ohio, last we heard."

"Ohio." I stop to think about that. "Do you ever see him?"

Emmitt shakes his head and keeps his eyes firmly glued to the road. "We never see him. He left when I was thirteen and Casey was eleven. Just took off. Got remarried and had new kids and everything. He calls once in a while to see how we are. Casey quit hockey that year, and we never talk about him. Just another statistic, that's what that is."

"Sorry, man." Which is a pretty stupid response, but I don't know what else to say.

We're quiet for a few moments, and then I realize that Emmitt has just shared something huge about his life, and I've never told him anything about me that actually matters. I think about that for a moment before I decide to give it a shot. "Dude, I don't know if you know this already…. My dad not being around is kind of the reason we live with Jack now. So I really mean it. About being sorry."

The corners of his mouth turn up in a slight smile, but he doesn't respond. "Thanks, Dusty," he says softly.

The party has already started by the time Emmitt and I get there. Aaron's house is small but nice; it has a decent-size kitchen and a living room that spreads out lengthwise. The living room is covered with Halloween decorations, and liquor and beer bottles dot every inch of spare furniture space. The lights are off, and strobe lights and Halloween-themed party lights are hung up all around the room. Loud dance music is playing conspicuously in the background; looks like Aaron decided to go with the shuffle mix after all. A few people in the center of the room are dancing, and small groups of people are crowded in the corners of the room. Some people are in costume and some not. Most of the girls have on pretty skimpy outfits, and I see one girl from a few of my classes who's dressed an awful lot like Britney Spears—and I'm pretty sure that's not her costume.

Casey comes running up when he sees me. "Hey, dude," he whispers, as though he's on some kind of secret mission for the CIA. "Alicia's over there."

*Here we go again.* Sure enough, Alicia is standing in a corner surrounded by girls, drinking something out of a blue party cup. Casey keeps poking me. "Head over there, man. She's got a curfew, I think—she won't be there forever."

I just glare at him, wondering where that James Dobson book is when I really need it. "I will, okay? Just give me a minute."

Emmitt, from behind me, cracks up. "Ooh, is the party making somebody nervous?"

I mean, how much crueler can life get? Really? I glare at them both, trying hard to ignore how amazing Emmitt looks in his hockey jersey (I guess it's supposed to be his costume or something) with his eyes all lit up and happy. "I think... I need a drink or something," I say before I charge to the kitchen.

The problem is that I'm not sure what to do once I get there. There are a whole lot of bottles on the table and a keg of something in the corner, and all of it looks totally unfamiliar. I know, it's weird—my dad spends most of his time above a bar and I've never even had a sip of beer. Except the reason it happened that way is that he spent so much time above that bar that I never had time to do much besides raise his kids. With that angry thought high in my mind, I pour a few ounces of something clear into a cup and take a slug.

"Ack!" I run to the sink and immediately spit most of it back out as Emmitt walks into the room, shaking his head.

"Dusty, what is wrong with you? Vodka? Straight up?"

I glare at him again. "I just wanted to try something," I mumble miserably. Apparently we can mark drinking down as one more thing I fail at.

He starts mixing together the disgusting clear stuff with a bunch of juices, and soon he hands me a cup that doesn't smell at all nauseating. "Try this. I put a lot of juice into it. You should barely even taste the vodka."

I take a sip. He's right; it's actually drinkable. "Much better. Thanks."

"Least I can do." He slaps me on the shoulder. "That should give you the courage to go in there and talk to Alicia."

Maybe it's the sip of vodka, or the fact that the James Dobson book I seem to so desperately need hasn't shown up yet. Maybe it's

93

just that I'm tired of pretending to be something it's becoming pretty clear I'm not. Either way, I decide it's time to say something. "Yeah… about that. I'm actually not really into Alicia." I take another sip.

Emmitt pumps something from the keg (beer, I'm pretty sure) into a cup of his own and comes back to stand beside me. "Dusty, why didn't you say something to Casey? He's practically got you married off already."

I'm struggling to come up with an answer to that when he slaps me on the shoulder again. "No big deal. I mean, you haven't even talked to her yet. Are you into someone else? Let's get more of that shit into you and find out who."

As bad an idea as that probably is, I go along with it and chug some more of the mysterious contents of my cup.

Emmitt leads the way out of the kitchen and back into the living room, where Casey has found his way into a conversation with the Britney Spears girl. Good. At least he's distracted.

A few of Emmitt's hockey buddies come over, and we end up talking to them for a few moments. They're pretty cool, but one of the drunker ones can't seem to get past how much I look like Jack. "You're like… a mini him!" he keeps saying over, guffawing and laughing like Jules when she watches *SpongeBob*. It's almost enough to make me throw up whatever I'm drinking.

"Sorry about him," someone else in the crowd says. "But it is kind of weird, ya know. How much you look like him. You gonna play hockey?"

They're disappointed when I tell them I don't even know how to skate, and Emmitt's, like, shocked.

"Dusty, you can't even skate? We gotta fix that right away. You can't be Jack Morton's look-alike and not know how to skate."

I've spent most of the evening ignoring everything that happened right before Emmitt picked me up, and that one statement throws me right back to it all. "Why does everyone keep trying to make me his freakin' son? I have a father, you know. He may not be around or anything, but I do have one."

To give Emmitt credit, he looks flustered for less than a second before he responds. "Hey, man, I'm sorry. I didn't mean it like that." I must still look pretty annoyed, because he's quick to add, "Dusty, dude, you know I get that. I do."

I nod. I know he does. "It's just… it's that arm's-length thing you said about Casey, you know? Maybe he and I get along because I've kind of been the same way for a long time. People let you down, you know? Maybe Casey and I both figured that out, and that's what makes it okay for us to be… friends or whatever." I have no idea if any of this is making any sense or if the cup I'm drinking out of is having its effect on me. "So I don't want everybody up in my world. Because people let you down. And Jack and Beth are all about making us a… family." I think I actually spit out that part, along with some juice, which probably ends up all over the carpet. "I have a family, you know? Jules and Matt and I, we were a good family. A great one, even. Now it's all… different. It's all wrong or something."

"Uh, Dusty? Did something happen tonight? With you and Jack? Is that why you changed your mind about the party?"

I must look like I'm about to bawl or something, because Emmitt suddenly drags me away from the noise in the living room and down the hallway.

We end up in Aaron's bedroom, which Emmitt claims is going to be fine with Aaron. We can still hear the music coming from down the hall, but it's distant now, muted. And Emmitt's sitting on the bed next to me. "You okay?" he asks.

I take another drink from my party cup, which probably isn't the best idea, and I nod. "Fine, I swear. I mean, thanks for getting me away from everyone for a minute. But I really am fine."

Emmitt looks into his cup. "You wanna talk about it?"

I do. I think I do. I realize I haven't actually talked to anyone about any of this stuff since I moved to Vermont. Maybe I should think about going to see Jack's stupid shrink. I guess I do keep people at an arm's length, just like Casey.

I start to spill out the whole damn story. I start with the first time my mom took off when I was ten, and I don't stop until I reach the scene in the kitchen with Jack and Beth. "I mean, it shouldn't be a big deal, you know? Him saying that word. He *is* my uncle, after all. But I just... I just...."

"You're not ready to give up your old life. Why should you be? Nobody asked you if you even wanted any of this."

Emmitt says it so quietly that it takes me a moment to register that he's just nailed down the exact problem. "Yeah, that's it. That's totally and completely it. How did you... how did you know that?" I'm more in awe of Emmitt than I've ever been before, and that's saying something.

He smiles a little, sadly, and still we're sitting next to each other on Aaron's bed, and I'm not drunk, but I've had just enough alcohol that the impossible seems somewhat possible, and I'm leaning toward him, and he's leaning toward me—and then we're kissing, and it's like nothing I've ever felt before.

It's the first time Julia reached for me after a nightmare, and the first time Matt ever scored a goal in soccer, and the day in the park with my parents from so long ago, and the first time I stood on a skateboard, and that first taste of Jack and Beth's fried chicken, and the first time I ever listened to a complete Led Zeppelin album... all rolled into one amazing press of Emmitt's lips to mine.

It lasts a few moments, and then we pull away from each other, both of us panting, even though that kiss couldn't have lasted more than ten seconds. "Uh," I say. So much for expressing how life changing that was.

Emmitt doesn't have time to say anything because Casey is suddenly yelling for him, loudly, and Emmitt pulls open the door to the room and starts charging down the hall. I go charging after him. A large crowd has gathered at the front of the house, and guess who's at the center of it: Rick, waving a beer bottle around and pointing it intermittently at people. He looks completely smashed. A couple of his cronies from class stand behind him. "Whaddidya think, pretty boy?" He gestures the bottle at Emmitt. "That I wouldn't finoutabou' you taking my position this year?"

Casey is standing to the side of Emmitt, who, with his arms crossed, is rolling his eyes at Rick. "We've known that was going to happen since you got kicked off, Rick. I thought you didn't care about our stupid team. Isn't that what you said in the locker room the day Coach told you to get lost?"

The crowd makes some noises at that, and a few people back away from Emmitt. Rick moves closer and shoves him in the chest. "You think you can take my place? You... trash, man," he slurs. "Canna play for shit. Gonna suck this year, just like las' year."

Emmitt's look is gradually getting darker and darker, and I'm pretty sure it's not going to be too long before he finally hauls off and punches Rick.

"Rick," Emmitt snarls, "you think I give a crap what you say? Anyway, you and I both know you're just pissed that I was outplaying you, and that I was going to get the starting position this year whether you were still on the team or not." Now the music is no longer an upbeat dance track, and the loud heavy metal suddenly playing in the background sounds ominous, like a soundtrack in a bad movie.

Rick curses loudly. "My boys and I are gonna take you and your stupid party." He glances to his left and sees me for the first time. "Starting with that pretty boy nephew of Morton's." Now he waves his beer bottle at me. "You think I dunno who you are? I always know," he slurs.

Emmitt's in front of me so fast I actually have to blink at the air rushing by me. "Leave Dusty out of this, you asshole."

"Ooooh!" Ricky and his friends start slapping drunken high fives. "Little Morton got himself a protector!"

"Shut the hell up, Rick," Casey says from behind me. "There's only three of you guys, and you're all wasted. Just get outta here."

Rick howls with laughter. "Yeahhhh...," he slurs again. "I'm really worried about being beaten by a hippie skateboarder and my wimpy, retarded ex-hockey coach." He sways on his feet and stares at me, and I'm not sure if he thinks I'm Jack or something, but it doesn't really matter. All that matters is his last statement.

I'm not really sure why that last statement suddenly has me charging out from behind Emmitt, yelling, "What'd you call my uncle?" Maybe it's the vodka. All I know is that now I'm face-to-face with Rick, and Emmitt looks totally freaked out by my sudden challenge. Good. Maybe that means he's okay with the fact that I attacked his face with mine in his bedroom a few minutes ago.

"You heard me, punk," spits Rick. "The asshole hockey coach ruined my career." He drops his beer bottle and curses again. "Everyone in this town knows whatta dumbass he is, anyway. The day he cut me from the team, they all knew that."

I'm strangely proud to say that I throw the first punch.

It's a good one, too, right in the gut. Rick keels over for a second, and in that second the place goes nuts. Rick's goonies go after Casey and Emmitt, and Rick is throwing punches at my head while I try to get him in the stomach (it's pretty much all I can reach), and I'm pretty sure the rest of the party is in chaos— everybody is either trying to get out of there as quickly as they can or get in on the punching.

Rick gets me a few times in the face before Casey shoves him off, and I realize he and Emmitt pretty much have the goons (who I don't think were too sober to begin with) incapacitated. But Rick, drunk as he is, is still going at all three of us, so I keep throwing punches as long as I can.

Until someone pulls my arms behind me, and I realize that someone is wearing a police officer's uniform.

THE RIDE in the cop car is silent. Casey and I are in the back, Emmitt is in the front, and none of us are saying anything.

The police station is small, which is pretty much what I expect from a town this size. The inside doesn't look anything like police stations do on TV, but it's still pretty intimidating. The lighting is low and police officers are everywhere, filling out paperwork, talking on phones. Our cop, Officer Wozcoski, brings Casey, Emmitt, and me back to a claustrophobic little room where he sits us down and asks us our names.

He nods at Casey and Emmitt as they give theirs, and I get the impression he already knows who they are—small town syndrome, I suppose. Then I tell him my name.

"You're not related to Jack Morton, are you?" This guy is huge, and I am not about to lie to him.

"Yeah," I mumble. "He's my uncle. I live with him."

"Ah," mutters the cop. "The prodigal sister's child returns." I have no idea what that means, but I also don't really care.

He leaves, and Emmitt drops his head down onto the table with a sigh. Casey punches him in the shoulder.

"You freaking out about your season?"

Emmitt nods slowly. "If they press charges... there is no way Mom or Coach will let me play this year. It'll totally wreck my chances with college scouts."

A shot of guilt hits me. This is my fault. I started all this. I punched Rick. Sure, I'll get in trouble, but I don't really care what Jack does to me. What's the worst that can happen to me? But Emmitt could lose hockey over this.

"I'm so sorry, guys," I mutter. "I shouldn't have punched that dick. I don't know what I was thinking."

Emmitt looks up, shocked. "Dusty, what are you talking about? He insulted Coach. If you hadn't hit him, I would've. Especially after all that other crap he said about me taking his spot. Everybody knows he got kicked off for smoking too much dope. Besides, Dusty, you gotta fight for your family."

I open up my mouth to answer, but I don't have anything to say. I try to tell myself that I was really just defending Emmitt, but there's no denying that I punched Rick after he made that crack about Jack. The whole thing doesn't make any sense. I'm stuck on that point when Casey sighs. "Yeah, Dusty," he adds, "He was talking smack about your uncle. You had to punch the dude."

Defending Jack. Why would I do that? As Emmitt pointed out earlier, this isn't my family, and I got shipped out here without anyone even asking my opinion. Why had I hit Rick, anyway? Especially after what Jack said tonight.

Except that Jack and Beth had taken the three of us in when we had nowhere else to go.

And bought us clothes.

And food.

And the kids really like them.

And I look just like Jack.

And I still have that picture of my dad in my head, telling me he couldn't come back to the hospital with me.

Casey leans over and slugs me. "Hey, dude, where did you disappear to during the party? Did you finally hook up with Alicia?"

Emmitt and I exchange a furtive glance before I shake my head. "Uh… not exactly."

Casey sits up excitedly. "So where did you go? Who'd you hook up with?"

Now Emmitt is squirming uncomfortably, and I'm annoyed that he even *thinks* I would rat him out. "Oh, just talked to some other girls. Ya know, in the kitchen and whatnot. Nothing very exciting."

Casey sinks back down in disappointment, and Emmitt catches my eye and winks, as usual. That wink somehow makes me think maybe I can get through the uncomfortable conversation I'm pretty sure Jack and I are about to have.


BY THE time Jack comes roaring into the station, I can feel one of my eyes turning black, and Emmitt confirms it's going to be at least that color. "Is there anything darker than black?" he tries to joke, so I get that it looks pretty bad. My head doesn't feel too great either, and my gut, where I took a few hits from somebody, also isn't in the best shape. Casey and Emmitt have their fair share of bruises too, but I'm still betting Rick looks worse.

Jack is preceded by Officer Wozcoski into our little holding room. He's practically snorting fire. He looks us all up and down. "You three all right?"

We all just nod. There's a woman behind him who's basically a shorter female version of Emmitt, and it only takes my high IQ a few seconds to figure out she has to be Casey and Emmitt's mom. She spends a few moments hugging Casey and Emmitt and checking them over for bruises before Emmitt finally introduces us. "Mom, this is our friend, and Coach's nephew, Dusty. Dusty, this is my mom, Alice."

We shake hands, and she never stops staring at my black eye. It's definitely not the best introduction I've ever had to a friend's parent, let alone the parent of a guy I just made out with.

Now that the parents have arrived, the officer sits down to take our statements, asking a lot about what Rick said and what time he arrived. Emmitt tells everyone that Rick has been hassling me for weeks. When the officer asks who started the "physical altercation," as he puts it, Emmitt carefully avoids my eyes and answers.

"Honestly, I'm not really sure, sir. It all happened so fast. Everyone was just standing in a circle around us; it could have been anybody."

It's weird to hear him lie to a cop, but I guess it shouldn't be. As honest as he is, Emmitt has never struck me as the type to sell out a friend.

I try not to work up too much hope that this means he liked what happened between us in Aaron's bedroom as much as I did.

After listening to our statements, the officer leaves for a few moments. There are a lot of things I want to say to Emmitt, but I'm not about to say them with everyone else there.

The door flies open when Officer Wozcoski returns. "Well," he says, "the statements of others at the party support what these three have said. It looks like we won't be pressing charges against them." Emmitt lets out such a huge breath it's amazing he doesn't completely deflate.

"Jack," I mutter, "Emmitt's not off the team, is he?"

Jack didn't say much while we were giving our statements, but you can tell he isn't very happy. "Emmitt, I can honestly say that I'm pretty disappointed with most of the team right now, since it sounds like most of you were in on this fight. Still, I know how Rick's been since he was kicked off the team. This subject will definitely come up at our first team meeting, and I will definitely be talking to you and the other players about it, but I don't think I'll have to ask any more of you to leave the team. Thank goodness."

Emmitt's complexion improves about six shades, making me glad I asked. Jack says good-bye to Emmitt and Casey's mom and crooks his finger at me, no longer even looking at Emmitt and Casey. I can tell Emmitt wants to say something to him, but he seems to think better of it.

The truck's cold, but I'm not shivering. Jack drives quickly, and neither of us says anything for a while. He's the one who speaks first. "Dusty," he finally says, "I don't understand what happened tonight." He sounds almost sad. "Beth and I actually came back to the house with the kids early, because we were worried you might feel left out of the evening, and you weren't there. Now, I'm relatively new at having kids in my house, but I think I had five heart attacks just wondering where you were." His voice drops even lower. "Then, I get a call from the police, saying you were found at an extremely loud house party in a group fight with some of my ex- and current hockey players. *Then* they tell me that the fight was started by one of said ex-hockey players, who has apparently been hassling you for weeks, which you have never even mentioned to me. Can you explain any of this? At all? Why would you take off without even leaving us a note? Why didn't you ever say anything about Rick? What the hell is going on, Dusty?"

I blink back something that might be tears, but I can't see how. None of this makes any sense. No adult has really talked to me like this since Mom started disappearing, and I don't even know how to react. "Whatever," I mumble.

Jack pulls the truck over. "Why, Dusty?" he asks, and once again, I turn to the window so I don't have to look at him. "Why did you do it? You could have asked me if you could go. I don't know if I would have said yes or no, but you could have asked. Why all of it? Why not tell me about Rick? And why let yourself get pulled into that fight? Are you hoping to get me fired on top of everything? Do you hate me that much?"

The thing is, he's not really yelling at me or anything. He never even raises his voice at all. But even so, that line pisses me off. I know he doesn't know what happened in the fight, but he should figure it out—he has to know that Rick's been hassling me because of him. "I just want you to leave me alone!" I snap, even though I'm still not looking at him.

I hear Jack sigh. "Dusty…," he says, "I am trying to do the best I can here, for you and Matt and Julia. But you have got to talk to me. You have got to give me something to work with."

I don't have any answer for that, so I don't say anything.

Jack turns the car back on. "This can't keep happening, Dusty," he says very quietly. Then he goes on about how I clearly need to try some counseling, and how hard he and Beth are trying… blah blah blah.

I turn to look out the window again. He's right. This can't keep happening.

# CHAPTER SEVEN

*TWO YEARS Earlier*

*The knock on the door was unexpected. Race had gone home after school, so it couldn't be him, and none of Dusty's other friends ever came to their apartment. Checking to make sure that Matt and Julia were busy working on their homework at the table, Dusty went to answer the door.*

*"Hellooo!" Mr. Ludley, their landlord, was a decent guy, if eccentric. Dusty smiled at his greeting, which seemed to match his balding head and the polka-dotted tie he liked to wear. "Mr. Porter!" Mr. Ludley grinned. "Is your mother in?"*

*Not for over two weeks, Dusty thought snidely in his head. This was the longest she'd been gone so far, and there was almost no money left. Dusty had already decided that if she wasn't back by tomorrow, he was going to go to the place where he knew their father was staying and beg him for money. "Uh, she's still at work."*

*"Oh." Mr. Ludley frowned intensely. "Dusty... you know I enjoy chatting with your mother very much...."*

*Of course you do, thought Dusty. His mom would flirt and charm and get Mr. Ludley to give her extra time on the rent without him even noticing. Dusty found the whole thing disgusting.*

*"But she had promised the rent would be paid by now, and I still haven't received the check."*

*Dusty felt his skin clamming up. His mom hadn't paid the rent yet? It was nearly the end of the month. "Oh, sorry, sir. I bet she forgot. You know how she can be sometimes." He tried to laugh at his own joke, but he found himself almost coughing halfway through.*

*"True, true, I know she's a touch forgetful... not unlike me! Listen, I'll check back with her tomorrow, okay?"*

*The door closed, and Dusty ran to the bathroom to throw up. "Dusty?" Matt called after him. "Dusty, are you okay?"*

THE NEXT *day after school Dusty and Race sat outside Prescott, watching Matt play with a friend on the swings. Julia was inside at a minicarnival the school was having for the littlest kids, probably gorging herself on chips and juice. At least, Dusty hoped she was. Dinner that night was going to be slim pickings.*

*"I'm thinking of talking to your mom," Dusty said in a low voice.*

*Race glanced around to make sure no one else was listening. "You mean... about your mom taking off again?"*

*Dusty nodded, feeling his face go red. He was worried he was going to cry or something stupid like that. "I, uh, found out yesterday that my mom never paid the rent this month. And we're almost out of food. And it's been almost three weeks. I don't know where she is. And I haven't been sleeping much."*

*Now a tear did slip, but Dusty wiped it away quickly and Race tactfully ignored it. "Yeah, Dusty," Race sighed. "Maybe you need...."*

*"Dusty!"*

*Julia came racing out of the school, holding out a large creation of yarn and Popsicle sticks glued to paper. "Look what I made today!"*

*She bounced up and down excitedly; now Dusty could be sure that she'd had plenty to eat at the carnival. He took the picture from her and studied it.*

*The Popsicle stick figures were labeled, in shaky handwriting, DUSTY, MATT, and JULIA. The yarn around them formed smiles on their faces and a huge sun in the sky. At the corner of the picture it said, in the same shaky handwriting, "MY FAMLY."*

*"I'm going to go play with Matt, okay?"*

*Julia ran toward the playground, and Dusty watched her grab for Matt as she reached him at the jungle gym. Matt began to help her climb the wooden bars on one side of the contraption, and Dusty turned back to Race.*

*"Never mind, dude. I can't do it. I can't. I'll go see Dad tomorrow or something, get money from him. Mom has to come back soon anyway, right?"*

*Race still worried, sometimes, about Dusty's temper, about being the one to push him over the edge he always seemed so close to. So he didn't say what he wanted to say. Instead, he just said, "Sure, Dusty."*

THE SUN wakes me up early the next morning. My eye and my head hurt, but that isn't bothering me nearly as much as thinking about the night before. Everything about it was insane. Me beating up Rick over Jack. Jack screaming at me in the car. Me screaming back. Me and Emmitt… well, something.

I haul my sore body out of bed. It feels like a million years since I've seen Matt or Julia, and I wonder if Jack or Beth have told either one of them what happened.

The floor below the attic is completely empty, so I figure everyone is already up and having breakfast. Sure enough, they are all sitting around the table like one big happy family.

"Dusty!" Julia exclaims. "What happened to your eye?"

So nobody has told them. "Nothing, Julia. Just a fight."

Matt's staring at me, wide-eyed. I guess Beth notices, because she quickly changes the subject. "Eggs, Dusty?"

"Steak for your eye?" Jack adds dryly, handing me an ice pack from somewhere.

Is that supposed to make me laugh? I don't know what to say, so I just nod at Beth and hold the ice up to my aching face. "Yeah, eggs would be great." I sink into the chair next to Matt.

"Dusty," Julia asks as Beth dishes out a huge pile of scrambled eggs onto my plate, "why would a fight make your eye purple?"

Matt rolls his eyes. "It's called a black eye, stupid," he says knowingly. "It's what you get when someone punches you in the face."

I freeze in my seat. Did Matt just call Julia stupid?

"Matt, don't call your sister names," Jack says mildly. He leans over to Jules, "I know it looks purple, honey, but Matt's right. We call it a black eye." Julia sticks her tongue out at Matt, and everyone goes back to eating normally.

Except me. I mean, what's going on here? Matt and Julia, who have always gotten along really well, are fighting about Halloween costumes and calling each other names at the breakfast table?

After breakfast is over and Matt and Jules have been shooed off to clean their rooms, I decide to ask Beth what's going on. I'm not about to say two words to Jack if I don't have to.

Beth tosses me a concerned look as I follow her to the sink. "Hon, do you want some aspirin? That can't feel very good."

I accept the aspirin and choke it down. "Um, Beth? Matt and Julia seem to be fighting a lot lately."

Beth looks shocked. "I've hardly seen them fight at all, Dusty," she replies.

What is wrong with this woman? "Matt just called Julia stupid," I intone, trying not to raise my voice. "They never called each other names before." *Before we got here*, I add in my head.

Beth glances at Jack, who appears to be silently observing our conversation from the other side of the kitchen. "Dusty, the way they're behaving doesn't really seem out of the ordinary for siblings... that's the way most brothers and sisters act."

107

"Dusty," Jack suddenly interrupts from across the room, "I get the sense that Julia and Matt tried a little harder to watch their behavior in Colorado. When they knew they… had to."

What's he talking about? Sure, Matt helped me take care of Julia, and sure I'd needed them to get along to make sure we never got caught—but does that mean they don't really like each other, that it was all an act?

"Dusty, I think the kids are just less afraid to act like themselves now," Beth adds, as if she can read my thoughts. "I don't think it's that they feel any differently about each other than they used to."

I know what she's trying to say—that the kids are more secure here; that's why they can call each other names and be rude now. Because they don't have to worry the way they used to.

Why is that supposed to be a good thing? Why am I supposed to be happy that my brother and sister now have enough security to hate each other?

I'm not. And I don't want to be. I put my dish in the sink and take my ice pack up to my room, hoping a nap will somehow help any of this make sense.

I'M PRETTY sure, based on the light coming through the curtains over my windows, that it's late afternoon when someone knocks on my door and pulls me back into consciousness. "Whatisit?" I mutter sleepily.

"Dusty, Emmitt dropped by to talk to Jack and you. Is it okay if I let him in?"

I sit up instantly, all too aware that my hair is probably sticking up in fourteen different directions and I'm still wearing the same rumpled T-shirt I was wearing last night. Oh well. Not much use trying to do anything about it now—not if he's already at the door. "Uh, sure," I call back, trying to sound at least a little bit awake.

Emmitt comes in and immediately closes the door behind him, and I can't believe how excellent he looks for someone who went through the same thing I did last night. He's in jeans and a polo, and his hair is actually washed and dried. He has a faint bruise across the bottom of his jaw, but that's the absolute only clue that he wasn't just hanging out and watching movies last night.

"Hey, man. Sorry to wake you up." He sits on the end of my bed, and I stretch, hoping to get myself a little more alert for whatever conversation we're about to have.

"No problem. It's probably late anyway, huh? So, what's up?"

He glances around my nearly blank canvas of a room, concentrating on a University of Vermont pennant Beth must have hung there. "Not much. Talked to Aaron this morning. He's, like, grounded for life, but I don't think his parents are going to make him quit hockey."

"That's good, I guess. You talk to Jack?" I can basically feel my eyes narrow when I say that.

"Yeah, we're cool. It's like I told you. He knows how Rick is." He brings his eyes back to me. "He seems a little pissed that you didn't tell him Rick's been after you since you got here."

I can't keep the annoyance out of my voice. "He made that pretty clear last night."

Emmitt runs a hand through his hair, and it's almost all I can do not jump across the bed to get closer to him. "Look, Dusty, I get why this is hard for you and all. I do. I really do. Just... give Jack a chance if you can, okay? He's only upset because he wishes he could have helped you out."

Now, for the second time in twenty-four hours, I find myself getting pissed off with Emmitt. "Doesn't sound like you understand."

Emmitt shrugs. "I know how complicated it is, and I really do understand why you feel the way you do too. Just trying to help you see things from both sides." He sighs. "I didn't really come here to talk about that anyway. Can we... can we talk about the other thing that happened last night?"

The tone of his voice isn't very encouraging. "Yeah, yeah. Of course we can."

Emmitt scoots up the bed a little closer to me, and I can feel his hot breath—which smells like wintergreen gum—on my cheek. "Dusty," he says softly, "I really like you. A lot. I got the impression last night you like me too."

I snort. "Uh, yeah. Glad you noticed."

"I mean… I don't know how many other guys you've kissed. That was actually only my second time."

I'm not sure what to say to that. For some reason, I don't really want to tell him that was my first time kissing a guy—my first time kissing anybody ever, actually. Luckily for me, Emmitt keeps talking, and I never have to respond.

"That kiss last night… it meant a lot. I think you and I… I think we'd be great together."

I have a moment of triumph. Eight or so quick seconds of it, actually. Then Emmitt goes back to talking.

"But I don't think we can be."

And then he keeps talking.

"I mean, this is northern Vermont, Dusty. People just don't get that kind of stuff here. I don't know what it's like in Colorado—I've heard it's even worse, actually—but if people found out, that would be, like, the end for us. You think Rick hassles you now? You haven't seen anything. I'd have to quit hockey. I don't even know what Casey would say."

"So he doesn't know. About you." I say it really softly, because my voice doesn't seem to be working all that properly.

"No. He doesn't. I almost told him, after I kissed a guy at hockey camp last summer. But I couldn't, because I realized that I couldn't… couldn't *be* this. Couldn't be what I want to be. Couldn't be with who I want to be with."

He shakes his head. "I want to be, Dusty. I do. I just can't be. I'm really sorry."

He stands up to leave, and I find that, once again, I don't have anything to say.

As he closes the door behind him, I sink back onto the bed, wondering what's supposed to happen now. Do I accept that I couldn't make it up the mountain and move on? Settle in for a life with Beth and Jack raising my brother and sister, while I hang out on the side? See Emmitt at my locker every day, eat lunch with him, walk to classes with him and Casey, and pretend forever that last night never happened?

No. I don't want any of that. I don't want to be a wingman in a fake family. I don't want to keep searching for a way to learn to be something I'm not.

I realize that what Jack said last night was right—"This can't keep happening, Dusty," he'd said. For once, I totally agree with him. This can't keep happening. Everything went wrong the moment I stepped on that stupid plane in Colorado Springs.... That's the moment I need to undo.

So that's when I decide to do it.

I decide to go back to Colorado Springs to find my mom. Not because I need her. I don't. The kids don't. We gave up on her years ago. But I am going to have to find her and get her to convince the courts that the kids and I should live with her again. We can go back to our old apartment, she can come and go as she pleases again, and everything can go back to the way it was. After all, Julia can't get appendicitis twice, can she? I'll go back to being so busy taking care of Matt and Jules that this stupid problem of who I like and who I don't like won't even matter anymore, just like it didn't used to matter.

I'll get to be who I was again. I'll get to go back to living a life I had pretty well conquered.

JACK AND I continue our pattern of barely speaking for the whole next week. Jack has either forgiven me or just decided not to talk with me again about Halloween, because he's still really friendly, and he still spends most of our car rides home asking me how my day was. I'm still not giving him much to work with. I'm technically grounded, but all that really means is that I can't go to the skate park with Casey after school. If Jack has a late meeting, I have to sit in the library and do my homework. Nothing really changes with Emmitt, just like I thought it wouldn't. We still hang out at my locker, eat lunch together with Casey, walk to class together sometimes.

Sometimes I catch him looking at me with that same intense gaze he had locked on me in the bedroom that night, but I don't return it or even think much about it. Nothing can come from it, so what's the point?

The only silver lining of life is that Rick is nowhere to be found. According to the grapevine he's serving some time in juvie. Apparently he violated the terms of his probation on Halloween night. I'm not crying over his absence.

Still, that's the *only* thing I have going for me right now. I know I need to make a move soon. So I make plans throughout that entire week. I ask Jack, in the truck one day, if there is any news about Mom. Jack tells me that the cops have arrested some of Dad's friends for other things, but they haven't found Dad yet. He also says Mom still hasn't turned up, and she still isn't answering the last cell phone number we had for her. (I actually already knew that—I'd tried it a few days ago.) I figured Dad would be hard to find. If he's heard cops are looking for him, he can make himself invisible. But if Mom hasn't appeared anywhere yet, who knows where she is?

I decide my plan will be to get to our old apartment in Colorado and wait for her. I think she'll have to turn up there at some point to get her stuff if it's still there. If it's not, I'll start looking for her. If I find her, I can talk to her. Tell her what's going on. We can go to the cops together and she can ask for a second chance. The kids and I can go back to living with her.

The funny thing is that every time I refine this plan in my head, a little voice shouts *That'll never work—you know it'll never work! Don't be stupid!* All the flaws in it jump out at me over and over again. Where will I stay? That apartment could have someone living in it for all I know. What will I eat? I barely have any money. And speaking of having no money, am I really about to hitchhike all the way to Colorado? But what choice do I have? I've given up just taking what life throws at me and going with it. For once, I'm making a move for something *I* want—my old life.

My biggest worry is disappearing without saying anything to Matt and Julia. I have never been apart from them in their entire lives. The week after Halloween, it's almost torture to look at them. I know I am leaving, and I can't even tell them not to worry about me. What if they think this makes me just like our mom?

There's nothing I can do about that, so I try not to think about it too much. I figure I can call them along the way. I'm going to leave the cell phone Jack got me behind (I'm sure it's tracked or something), but I'll get calling cards and use pay phones or something.

Then it's the morning of the day I've decided to take off. Before school I dump all my books out of my backpack and fill it with a couple of shirts and underwear, warm gloves and hats, my huge winter jacket, as many granola bars and water bottles as I've managed to scrounge together, and all the money I have in the world. I shake my head at the scrawny amount. It's terrible. I'm definitely looking at a lot of hitchhiking. At least my black eye is pretty much gone; that would have definitely scared some potential rides off.

I plan to leave at lunchtime. Colby High is right near the highway, so it'll be easier to catch a ride from there than anywhere else. Plus, if I disappear at lunch, it probably won't get back to Jack that I'm gone until late in the afternoon. By that time, I'll be long gone.

As lunch period approaches, I start to get more apprehensive about this great plan of mine. What if something goes wrong? What if I can't find Mom? What if I never see the kids again? The nerves must show, because when Casey meets me at my locker between third and fourth period, he asks, "Dude, what's eatin' you?"

113

I know I shouldn't tell anyone, but I need to. I slam my locker shut hard. "Look, can you keep a secret?" I can feel myself start giving him Jack's "teacher" look, and his face contorts. He nods, though.

"Sure, man. You know I've got you."

"You can't tell anyone, Case. Not even Emmitt. And no way can you tell my uncle."

Casey, surprisingly, puts out his pinkie. "I never break a pinkie swear, Dust." His face is strikingly serious for someone using a gesture mainly held sacred by kindergartners.

"Well… okay." I hook pinkies with him. "I'm leaving, hitching out of here at lunch. I'm going to find my Mom."

"Whoa, that's pretty intense," hisses Casey, pulling his hand back. "Where are you going to go?"

"The Springs. She'll have to go back there eventually."

"You got any money?"

Casey's question startles me. "I don't know. Some."

Casey looks around the bustling hallway in every direction. The warning bell rings, and as crowds of kids around us start to pour in different directions, he reaches for his wallet and grabs out some bills. "Here, man. You might need this."

I momentarily flash to the time Race gave me money in the hospital to go find my dad. "Case, I don't know if I can take this," I murmur. At the same time, I know I want to. This is enough for at least some bus fare and food along the way. It'll make the trip ten times easier.

"Who cares?" Casey waves me off. "It's just money. But listen," he adds, leaning closer to me, "don't try too hard to find her, okay? Then you'd have to leave, and Emmitt and I really like having you around." With that, he disappears down the hallway, and I decide this is a better moment than lunch to make a good, clean exit.

I hike up yet another long, brown hill of Vermont to the highway and quickly catch a ride south to Burlington. The woman who picks me up is decent. She's a nurse at the hospital there. She

114

says she always picks up hitchhiking kids because she used to do it herself. She jokes with me a lot of the way and doesn't ask any questions about why I'm not in school. *Man*, I think, *if things keep going like this, this trip will be a breeze.*

She drops me off at the bus station in Burlington, and I reluctantly part ways with a large chunk of Casey's money to purchase a bus ticket to New York City. It's as far as I can get without going completely broke, and New York seems like it would be a good place to look for ways to head west. More people, more rides, right?

I eat some granola bars on the long bus ride and try to ignore the hunger pains in my stomach that catch me off guard when the guy next to me launches into a huge ham and turkey sandwich. It's a long ride, and I eventually nod off.

I wake up when the driver announces that we are heading into Port Authority Bus Station, New York City. *Too late to go back now*, I think, as I exit the bus and head into an old, dingy tunnel of the station.

I think it's important to mention here that the first time my mom and dad both disappeared at once, I never cried. Matt and Julia were really young then, and tough to take care of, and I was really young too, but I never once let myself lose it. I just found food for them and got them to daycare and school, and I never let them see how scared I was. But now I'm alone in the biggest city in the world (well, I'm not totally sure of that, but it sure feels like the biggest city in the world), and I am still too close to Jack and Beth's to call my brother and sister and tell them I'm okay. I've never been so lonely in my life. It takes everything I have to suck it up and head into the brighter lights of the station itself.

I decide that ignoring the disgusting bus bathroom all the way down here means a trip to the restroom is in immediate order. I head inside a long, narrow men's room and am right in the middle of doing my business when I look down and realize the backpack I set down next to me has disappeared.

I take a few deep breaths so I don't pass out. Great. Great great great. I've been stupid enough to put everything I had with me into that backpack—my wallet, all the money Casey gave me. Everything.

So much for thinking a boy from Colorado Springs could survive in the big city.

"Hey!" I yell out, panic taking over my voice. "Hey! Who grabbed my backpack? Who took it?" People in the huge restroom stare at me, confused, and it occurs to me that whoever jacked my bag is probably long gone. It also occurs to me that if I keep yelling like this, I'm going to attract the attention of a lot of strange adults, and that's the last thing I need right now.

I practically race out of the restroom to look around, but I'm immediately engulfed in a crowd of people, and there is definitely no one in that crowd standing around holding my backpack. I slink over to a nearby chair and sit, because I have absolutely no idea what else to do.

I start feeling around the pockets of the coat I'm wearing, just to see what assets I still have. Nothing. I feel around my jean pockets. No money, not even any change.

Okay, this is probably the point where Zeb turned back and started to hike down the mountain. But I'm not Zeb, and I haven't done enough research yet to see if that whole "turning around" thing was even his idea. So I decide I'm not going to let this stop me. I mean, it's not like I had a whole lot of money to begin with anyway.

I venture out of the bus station into bright lights. And I mean bright. I've spent my entire life in a small city and a very small town, and neither one has really prepared me for how many lights there would be here.

Or how many people.

They're everywhere. I start heading right (it's a 50/50 shot, right?), and I'm immediately in the middle of and/or in the way of about three hundred people. Again, that might be a slight exaggeration, but it sure feels that way.

I don't know how long I walk, entranced by the tall buildings and lit billboards around me, before I hear, "Hey man, you got any money?"

Here's the thing: it's not like I've never seen a homeless person before. Check out Acacia Park in Colorado Springs sometime; it's basically a shelter. It's just that I've never seen quite this many in one place.

There are probably thirty people homeless people just sitting around. Some are wrapped up in newspapers, and one or two have filled shopping carts next to them. Most look older, even though I don't think they are all that old. One woman's face is lined like she's fifty or sixty, but her eyes tell me she might not be more than thirty.

And the guy who asks me for money? He can't be much older than Emmitt.

My stomach starts a churn. When younger homeless guys approached me in the Springs, it always made me nervous—not because I didn't like homeless people or something, but because I always knew how close I was to being where they were. Because every time Mom forgot to pay the rent, or the electric bill, or come home just before we ran out of food, I always felt like I was one step from having to keep Matt and Julia and me from either foster care or the streets.

I keep walking, because I find I can't look at the guy. Plus, it's not like I have any money anyway.

I suddenly don't know what I'm going to do now. What was I thinking, trying to hitchhike out of New York with no money or food? I may as well face the fact that if I keep going like I am now, I *will* end up just like that kid who just talked to me.

But I still can't bring myself to call Jack.

I frantically feel around my pockets again, looking for a couple of dollars I might have missed or something. I don't even find a quarter, but my fingers do nudge something rough in my back left-hand pocket.

That's pretty strange. I don't think I've even worn these pants since we got to Vermont. They're pretty old, and Beth bought me all new ones. These are the pants I'd been wearing on the flight out here.

When Jed gave me his card.

I tug out the battered piece of cardstock that's now been put through the wash. The water has smeared Jed's last name and address, but somehow his cell phone number has survived. Before I can think about it too hard, I start looking for a payphone.

It turns out that in this day and age, pay phones are hard to come by. I have to walk another, like, twelve blocks before I randomly see one in the entranceway of a diner.

I give up some dignity and ask a woman heading into the diner if I can borrow some money to make a phone call. It seems better to give up dignity now than to call this near-stranger collect.

"Jed Davies." The background noises make it sound like he's out at a restaurant or something. "Hey," I say, trying to pull my thoughts together. "You don't know me much, but I met you on a plane once."

Silence, and I started to worry I've made a huge mistake. "Plane? Who the hell is this?"

Suddenly I can't remember why I even bothered to call this guy. Even if he does remember who I am, isn't he just going to rat me out to my uncle and aunt? Then I remember his story, and I'm pretty sure he isn't going to do that. And what other choice do I have? I have no money, no food—nothing. "Dusty. It's Dusty. I didn't tell you my name, but I was traveling with my brother and sister. You said you had an aunt and uncle too." I realized that doesn't make much sense, but it's all I can seem to put together.

"Oh." I hear surprise in his voice, then irritation. "Kid, is there any particular reason you are calling me at nine o'clock at night?"

I blink. I haven't even realized how long I've been traveling. "Right," I sigh. "I'll go."

"Wait," he says crossly, just before I hang up. "Why are you calling at nine o'clock on a Tuesday?"

I try to figure out how to explain this mess I've gotten myself into. "I… tried to leave."

"Leave Vermont?"

"Yeah. I'm at...." I name the random diner I walked into. "Near 23$^{rd}$ Street."

"Okay," Jed says. He sounds like he can't believe he's having this conversation. "Okay. What are you doing there?"

"I was hitchhiking," I mumble. "Then I took a bus. I was going to keep going from here. But I got here and I was taking a piss and someone grabbed my backpack and it had all my money in it and now I'm not really sure what to do next...."

Jed sighs heavily. "Dusty, have you been doing drugs? Drinking?"

I shake my head a few times before I realize he can't see that. "Uh-uh. None of that. It's okay, Jed. Don't know why I called you. I'll just find a ride somewhere."

*"Find a ride?* More hitchhiking?"

When I don't answer, he laces in. "Do you have any idea how dangerous that is? Hang up the phone right now and call your uncle to get you."

Even in my dazed state, I'm appalled. "No way. It's like you said.... I was just starting to like him. He screwed it up."

There is a very long silence, and I'm starting to think Jed has hung up on me when he speaks again. "Dusty, you're at 23$^{rd}$ Street?"

"Yeah."

"You don't have any money for subway fare? You've probably never even been on a subway anyway, have you?"

"Ah... no."

"Shit. I'll have to come get you." He tells me to wait in the diner, and I get the sense he knows this area of town pretty well. "It'll take me awhile to get there. Sit tight. Don't leave, or I swear to God I will be so pissed I will come and find you."


"DUSTY."

Someone calls my name while I'm busy studying the signs next to the phone. (It's either that or tell yet another waitress that I don't need a table, I'm waiting for someone.) It's a voice I know.

119

Not well, but I know it. Jed. I turn slightly and find him standing there, a hand on my shoulder. "You ready to go?"

"Go? Where are we going?"

He gestures for me to follow him. "My place. It's already almost ten. We're not figuring this out in the middle of the street."

I should probably balk at the idea of going to a nearly complete stranger's house in a strange city, but where else am I supposed to go? Plus, I called him. I end all concerns by reminding myself that I was about to go hitchhike with complete strangers, so what's the real difference?

Jed hails a cab and urges me into it. He names off an address in Brooklyn and we spend the ride in silence, with me staring out the window as though as I am seeing a whole new world for the first time—because I pretty much am.

Eventually the car pulls up to the curb of a street lined with older, brick, skinny-looking houses. Jed hands the driver a wad of bills and leads me out of the car and up a steep set of stairs.

His apartment is on the third floor of the building. It's nice— he's got it painted an almost soothing beige color, and there are plants and paintings everywhere. Somehow I expected him to live in some disgusting bachelor pad.

"You want something to eat?" My face must answer that question, because Jed starts to laugh. "I'll order a pizza. You really haven't lived until you've had New York City pizza." He orders the pizza; then he sits down on one end of the couch in the small living room and gestures for me to sit on the other end. "So, my little runaway airline companion," Jed begins, "you wanna go into a little more detail about what's going on here?"

I scowl. "Not really. I mean, it's simple. I didn't want to go there in the first place. I hate it there. I just want my old life back."

Jed snorts at that. "Your uncle said you got into some kind of a fight over him."

I'm on my feet in about three seconds. "You called him? You told him where I am?"

120

Jed seems bemused by my reaction. "What, you think I just invite runaway teenagers into my home all the time without letting the authorities know where they are? Don't kid yourself, son. I had the Vermont police on the phone about two minutes after you called. Got to talk to your uncle a few minutes after that. I had to tell them where you are. Do you want me to get arrested or something?"

That pisses me off so much I start heading right for the door, but Jed's laughter stops me. "Dusty, what are you doing? Come back here. I'm not taking you back up there tonight. Chill out and have some pizza." He shakes his head, then mutters, almost under his breath, "God, you are exactly like I was."

I don't want to stay. I really don't. But the guy did just order pizza... and he did say he wasn't planning on taking me back tonight. I figure I can always take off later on, after I've had some food. It's not like I have any plans for the evening anyway, so I sit back down on the couch. "Some guy said stuff about Uncle Jack at a party. I hit him. I thought... maybe I liked Jack after all that. I was wrong about all of it."

"So you realized you liked your uncle a little. Then he tried to talk to you about it and you got pissed again?" Jed goes into the kitchen to grab us some sodas.

When I don't answer, he tosses me the soda from across the room. "Geez, Dusty, I realize you've never had any parent care enough to yell at you, but don't you realize that was your uncle being in charge of you? Watching out for you? Protecting you?"

"They don't care about me."

"Load of bull they don't. When I talked to your uncle tonight, he was worried as hell about you, praying you were okay. You think your parents were doing that tonight? Or ever?

"Listen, kid, I came to pick you up because the idea of you hitchhiking scared the bejesus out of me, and I knew that's what you'd do if I didn't come. And I came because I know how you're feeling—like you've lost control."

Somehow, I know he's exactly right. It's just like that moment I had with Emmitt in his bedroom. He's nailed down a problem I can't even begin to explain.

121

"Kid, what you don't realize is that you don't have to control everything anymore. You think you do, but you don't. You don't have to be in charge, controlling everything now, because there's somebody else there to help you when you get into stupid fights, somebody to wait up for you all night. You're not going to fall off the edge anymore.… There's a floor under you now when things go wrong."

I drop my head into my hands, because there's a chance I might start crying here, and there's absolutely no way I want him to see that. "It's just… it's not fair, you know? I was doing really well back there. I know it doesn't seem like it, but I was. I had everything figured out. Now I have to start all over again… and I didn't want any of this. I want my old family back. I want my old life back. And then, I want this other thing I can't have, and that just makes it even worse.… It's not fair." I am crying a bit now, and I really hope Jed somehow hasn't noticed.

He slides down the couch and sits next to me. "It never is, Dusty. It never gets fair. The best you can do—the best any of us can do—is to figure out when you're going in the wrong direction and find the right one. That's all you can ever do."

*Kind of like Zeb Pike,* I can't help but think. I have a feeling he's suggesting that I probably shouldn't have dealt with all this by trying to hitch my way across the country. "I don't know if I can do that."

"Well, okay. Look at it this way. You keep talking about how unfair it is that you had to leave Colorado and move in with your aunt and uncle, right?"

"Yeah, pretty much."

"Look at all the great new life opportunities they're presenting you with, if you'll just take them. They kept you out of foster care. They want to love you and do the best they can for you. They must be good with your brother and sister, or I know there is no way you would have left the two of them in Vermont."

Truth? This is everything I was thinking the night of the fight, as I was sitting in that station with Emmitt and Casey. He's right, I know he is. I just don't want to think about it right then.

"When's the pizza going to get here?" I ask.

# CHAPTER EIGHT

*FIVE MONTHS Earlier*

*It was a really good thing the school year was almost over.*

*That was all Dusty could think as the PE coach blew the whistle and Dusty dribbled the basketball back to the rack. If he had to take too many more PE classes watching Daniel do lay-ups, he'd probably have to leave Prescott and go find an all-girls school somewhere.*

*Dusty changed in the bathroom stall rather than by the lockers, carefully avoiding the awkward situation of seeing Daniel without a shirt on while other guys were around, and practically ran out of the gym to go find Matt and Julia.*

*He walked them home, listening to Julia babble on and on about the DVD their mother had promised to rent for them that night. Dusty tried not to get his hopes up too high; he knew it was 2:1 odds at best that their mom would even still be there when they got home.*

*Surprisingly, she was, and Dusty reveled in the way she curled up with Matt and Julia on the couch while he slunk back to his bedroom to try to get some sleep. His nose had been running all day, and his throat was starting to ache.*

*"Dusty! Dusty! We want breakfast!"*

123

*Dusty woke to a horrific headache, no ability to swallow, and Julia leaning over him. "Uhh... have Mom get you cereal, okay, Julia?"*

*"I can't, Dusty! She's not here."*

*Dusty groaned. He couldn't even remember the last time he'd felt like this; all he wanted to do was chug some NyQuil and go back to sleep. But someone was going to have to get Matt and Julia to school.*

*"Julia, get me the phone, okay?" Their dad's latest cell number was around somewhere. If Dusty called him, maybe he could come by long enough to take Matt and Julia to school. He hadn't seen them in almost a month anyway, so he probably wouldn't mind spending some time with them.*

*A moment later she was back with the cordless, and a few moments after that Dusty was remembering that his mom had stopped paying the bill a while ago, saying it was easier just to use her cell. She hadn't seemed worried that Dusty didn't have a cell phone of his own.*

*"I'm hungry, Dusty! I want eggs."*

*Dusty hauled himself out of bed and started searching for Kleenex. It was going to be a long day.*

THE PIZZA is really good, and it's late enough by the time we finish eating that Jed just throws me some blankets and pillows and tells me to sleep on the couch before he heads off to his bedroom. He doesn't mention anything about taking me back to Vermont, or seem even remotely worried that I'll take off in the middle of the night. I don't mention either point, as a good portion of me does plan on taking off in the middle of night.

It's only a portion, though, and as I lay down for what may just be a quick nap, I'm finding it really hard to ignore what Jed said.

I fall asleep thinking that, and when I wake up, Jack is sitting on the couch next to me.

"Shit!" I'm so surprised to see him sitting there, drinking a cup of coffee as though there is absolutely nothing strange about this situation, that I almost fall off the couch. No lie.

"Morning." He takes another sip. "How are you?"

That's the only thing he has to ask me? "Uhh... fine. You?"

"Well, I could be better. I did, after all, just take a very long train ride from northern Vermont to New York City. Thank goodness the train runs overnight, so I at least got some sleep." He takes another sip and gestures toward the bathroom. "Jed had to leave for work, but he said to help yourself to the shower. We're catching the train back to Vermont tonight, so you have plenty of time."

It's like I've stepped into some weird alternate universe. Who is this guy?

"Jack—"

"Dusty, why?" His interruption is so sudden that I can't help but look directly at him. "I realize you were upset about our fight in the car that night. I realize you haven't been very happy with us. But still.... I feel like this came out of nowhere. You still won't talk to me, Dusty. I had no idea you were upset enough to... to leave."

I stare at the couch again, because I'm not sure how to explain anything. As usual.

"Look, take a shower. As long as we're here, I may as well show you some of New York City. We've got plenty of time before the train."

TIMES SQUARE is... well, disgusting. Disgusting and amazing at the same time. It's like wall-to-wall people and stuff, and lights that are everywhere and are pretty impressive even during the day, and a lot of the tall buildings I saw the night before, and shopping in every direction.

And the food. Whew. Jack takes me to this place that is supposed to be famous for their cheesecake, but I personally think they should be famous for just about everything they make. I have never had a roast beef sandwich quite like this one, and I don't think I ever will.

We are gnawing on the amazing cheesecake when Jack brings up the subject we haven't discussed since that morning. "Can we try to talk now, Dusty? Are you finally ready to try and explain some of this to me?"

It doesn't feel like I can, but two other people have put it pretty well for me in the past, so I decide to borrow their words as much as possible. "It's just, well, I didn't want any of this, you know? I always wanted my mom to start acting like a mom again, or my dad to act like a dad, and that didn't happen, and then we got shipped out to Vermont and no one even asked me, does that make sense? It was like I was losing control, and it just felt really unfair. I'm used to being in control all the time, and now I wasn't, and *that* felt even more unfair…. Beth was taking care of the kids all the time and I never saw them. Not enough, anyway. And sometimes I even liked being able to, like, go to a Halloween party because I didn't have to take care of them, and that didn't seem right either. I got all confused."

"And then you stood up for me and you couldn't figure out why." He says it really quietly.

"Yeah, I guess."

"Look…," Jack starts. "I just want to make sure you know…. I wasn't mad at you that night." I nod, because really I already knew that, and Jack keeps going. "I was just upset that you hadn't told me what Rick was doing to you in school. Upset that you didn't trust me enough to ask me for help. I *was* mad that you took off without telling me, but only because I was worried about you. Why didn't you tell me, Dusty? About any of it? About what Rick was doing, or about what really happened at that party?"

I tap my fork against my plate and decide to tell him the truth. "Honestly?"

"Yeah. Honestly."

I shrug. "I think... I didn't want to need your help, or permission, or something. I didn't want to need anything from you."

Jack nods slightly, so I keep going. "Plus, I couldn't figure out why I hit him. I was so mad at you, but when he said that stuff... it just sort of came out." I thought for a second. "I think I may not have always hated you as much as I thought I did. I just...."

I can't seem to finish the sentence. "Still couldn't figure it all out," Jack finishes for me lamely.

"Yeah... maybe. I don't know. I guess we'll see." I don't want to make any promises I'm not sure I can keep.

Jack looks like he wants to say something else. Finally, he does. "Dusty, I know you've really resisted the idea of counseling, but would you consider it now? I think we all should have some, together. Matt and Julia seem to really benefit from having someone to talk to at their school. I think it would be good for all of us to talk to someone about the changes we've been through."

It hits me for the first time that Jack and Beth had their lives uprooted almost as much as the three of us did when we showed up on their doorstep. I'm still not sure how I feel about having to talk to someone about my feelings all the time—it was hard enough to do it with Emmitt on Halloween and with Jack today. But I don't want to ruin this decent moment Jack and I are having together, so I just say, "I'll think about it."

It's after Jack's paid the bill and we're walking around Times Square again that Jack mentions something I've been trying not to think about. "Emmitt... he was really upset when you ran off. More upset than I've ever seen him. Dusty, is everything okay between the two of you?"

I'm about to brush the question off with a quick "yeah" when Jed's words about changing directions come to mind. I still don't know if I really trust Jack, but this seems like a pretty solid way to find out. I'll never know if I don't give him the chance.

Plus, I have a weird feeling he *won't* let me down this time.

I concentrate hard on staring at a billboard in front of me. We're walking toward the ToysRUs store, because Jack said we need to take pictures of the giant Lego buildings for Matt and Julia (it sounds like he already promised to take them there someday), and there are people milling all around us. "Jack, I kissed him. And he kissed me. I guess… I guess I'm gay." It feels so strange to say that out loud… but not exactly wrong.

"Oh." Jack looks surprised but not stunned. He barely misses a beat, though, before he says, "Are you guys together?"

"Nah. He… didn't want to be. Said we can't be. That's probably also a little bit why I left."

Jack stops and tugs on my jacket sleeve until I stop too. He turns me so I'm looking directly at him. "Did your parents know?"

I scoff. "Jack, I wasn't even sure until Emmitt. I mean, I always knew something was different, but I didn't know for sure. Now I do."

"Oh." He smiles. "Dusty, Emmitt's a good kid. He'll do the right thing. If you like him and he likes you, I really don't think he'll let you down. You just may have to wait for him to figure out how to handle this. And just for the record… I'm really glad you told me. Thank you."

That's great and all, it really is, but it's not quite the biggest thing on my mind. "What if he doesn't? What if… what if he never figures it out?"

He puts his arm around my shoulder and starts leading me back up the street. "Then I'll kick 'im off my team."

THE SUNLIGHT spins lazily in the windows as I squint up. I'm in the attic room, closed inside the blue walls, and I'm surprised at how tired I still feel after sleeping most of the day. I didn't sleep much on the train last night, so Jack let me take another day off from school. I am so not looking forward to my waiting pile of makeup work.

I go downstairs for some juice and find Beth in the kitchen reading the newspaper. She's not smiling, but she isn't frowning either. I wonder what my facial expression looks like. "Look who finally woke up," she says. "Do you want something to eat?"

"Sure."

She bustles around the kitchen, putting together soup and a grilled cheese sandwich. Nobody's made me a grilled cheese sandwich in a long time—except maybe cafeteria workers. "Thanks," I say as she sets it down in front of me.

She disappears out of the room for a few minutes and returns with a large, red bag. "Jack and I got you something. I guess it's a welcome home present."

Who knew you can actually get presents for running away. I pull two boxes out and open them one at a time. Hockey skates are in one, and there is a brand-new skateboard in the other. "Uhh... thanks, I guess. I mean, thanks." I don't know what to say. The skateboard is the first one I've ever owned. It's perfect.

"Dusty... do you know why Jack and I never had any kids?" Beth's talking again, so I rip my eyes away from the skateboard to meet hers.

"I dunno," I say.

Beth nods, a half-smile crossing her lips. "We couldn't. It was all I ever wanted, all Jack ever wanted. But I can't. It's all me, Dusty. I'm the reason we can't have kids." Her eyes wander to the window, and I follow her gaze to the mountains there.

"Did you try adoption?" I ask.

She turns. "Yeah. But it's a long process. We were right in the middle of it when who should call us but someone saying we had two nephews and a niece who needed a place to live."

She smiles at me. "Dusty, I think you're a great kid. What you did for your brother and sister all those years...." She shakes her head. "It's amazing to me. I'm not trying to take any of that away from you. All I want is for you not to have to do that anymore."

"Yeah," I say, glancing over at my first skateboard and my first pair of ice skates. "Yeah." But that's all I can seem to get out.

Beth sits back on the edge of her chair. "Dusty, who did things for you? Who did all the things for you that you've been doing for Matt and Julia? Who even taught you how to do laundry and cook? Who took care of you when you were sick?"

It's honestly hard to remember. "I guess Mom when she was home…. When she wasn't… I just sorta survived, I guess. You know me. Get through anything."

Beth shrugs and stars clearing plates. "Maybe, Dusty," she smiles, "life could be about more than just surviving."

That's about as much talking about all this as I can take in twenty-four hours, so I decide another nap is in order. I wake even later in the afternoon to Matt jumping up and down next to me, with Jules hugging me desperately around the neck. "You came home! You came home!" Matt is shouting.

Home. I guess that's what these people and this scenery are now.

Matt laughs at something I can't—or don't—see. "We missed you! Where did you go?"

Julia lies down and settles under the crook of my arm. Matt sits down on the bed next to her, hands propping up his chin. They both wait patiently for my answer. "Well, I thought maybe I'd try to find Mom."

Julia looks confused. "Oh…. I thought Beth was our new mom."

Matt shakes his head. "'Course not, Julia. We still have our real mom too. Beth's just a replacement." He rolls his eyes at me as if to say, *Duh!*

"Well, Matt…." I take a deep breath. "I'm starting to think maybe Julia's right. Maybe it's about time you guys started thinking of Beth like a mom."

Matt is obviously surprised. "But I thought you didn't like Beth." Julia bobs her head in agreement.

I shift uncomfortably. "Well, I'm going to try to." I decide to leave it at that, because that is as simple as it is.

Matt frowns. "Yeah, that's good. I mean, Mom's always gone anyway…. I don't really remember what she looks like very well." He squints up toward the ceiling. "She had blonde hair, right?"

He barely remembers what she looks like. I hardly have time to process that before there is some creaking on the stairs, and Beth appears in the doorway. "Hey, guys, it's time for dinner."

Matt stands up and whoops loudly. "Meatloaf night!" He starts doing some ridiculous dance that I can only assume he learned from some TV show or something. "I love meatloaf… bring your beefloaf… let's get some meatloaf…."

And suddenly, I'm really happy I ended up back in this house.


"DUSTY, CATCH your edge, man."

I feel myself falling, but there is nothing I can do to stop it. The board is flipping under me. I hit the sidewalk hard, scrapes instantly forming on my bare palms as I plant them down to catch myself. I curse loudly, and Casey smacks his board hard against the ground, carefully bracing his knees before he makes contact. Skateboarding with him isn't doing much for my self-esteem.

At least it's less weird than hanging out with his brother. Emmitt and I haven't talked about anything that matters—at least to me—since I came back to school a few days ago. He's polite and all, always talks to me at the lunch table, but that's it. He seems pretty okay with pretending that nothing ever happened between us, which I guess proves that Jack really doesn't know everything.

I pull my jacket closer to my body. There's already some snow on the ground now, and even Casey the skateboarding maniac is going to have to give up boarding at the park pretty soon. "Geez," I say again, shuffling over to a swing set and leaning on it. "I haven't even had any real chances to practice, and it's already winter."

Casey shrugs and does a kick flip. "So? Doesn't mean you can't still keep practicing. I ice skate in the winter to keep my balance strong and stay in shape."

"Really? I thought you gave up ice skating a long time ago."

Casey concentrates hard on another kick flip as he shakes his head. "Nah. I gave up *hockey* a long time ago. But *skating* I will never give up. It's the reason I have such great balance on a board." He lands the trick, smacking into the ground with a kind of strange finesse I can only admire. "Really. You should ask Jack for a pair of ice skates."

I pull my board up to try another trick. "No sweat. I already have some."

"Good." Casey goes up for another trick. "Emmitt and I will take you to the rink Saturday. He's practicing like crazy now that the hockey season started anyway, and he will never forgive me if I try to teach you to skate without him." He lands the trick perfectly, smiling the whole time, and I don't have the heart to tell him that I think Emmitt would probably be just fine with me learning to skate on my own.

I'VE BEEN wrong about a lot of things lately, so I guess I shouldn't be too surprised when Casey calls me up on Friday night to tell me that Emmitt's really excited to go the rink with us the next day. I finally decide that either Emmitt's just trying to be nice or he doesn't want Casey to catch on that something's weird between me and him.

Jack drops me off. Within twenty minutes Casey's disappeared to hit on some figure skater, and I'm making a total ass of myself by trying to skate in front of Emmitt.

"I guess this really is your first time skating," Emmitt says as I try to figure out how to get to my feet on two crazy thin pieces of metal. Who invented this stupid sport, anyway? I grab hold of the wall, begging for it to help me.

"Shut up." I scowl at Emmitt, who's smiling as he skates backward. "C'mon, is anybody good at this the first time?" I finally get to my feet and propel myself forward, one foot at a time. I've only been on ice skates for two minutes, for cripes sake. Besides, it's already getting easier.

Emmitt is watching my feet with great interest. "Actually, Dusty, you're catching on to it really quickly. Maybe you'll be another skating prodigy, like Casey." He jerks his arm toward the other end of the ring where Casey is literally skating in circles around the figure skater, probably trying to convince her to go out with him. It doesn't look like it's going very well.

By now I've actually managed to glide forward, one skate edging into the ice at a time. Emmitt grins, impressed, and despite everything, that's all it takes to make me break into a grin. "Dude, that's way better. Coach must've passed it in the genes."

"Oh, he's that good, huh? I thought he was just a high school coach."

Emmitt slices his skates through the ice and stops to stare at me. "What? Just a high school coach? Did you know that Coach Morton almost single-handedly won Colby three state championships when he went to school here?"

Jack had? Really? "Nah, I didn't know that," I respond. "He was pretty good?"

"Good?" Emmitt looks incredulous. "Dusty, do you know anything about your uncle? He won all the high school MVP awards and had like a zillion college scholarship offers. He's a legend in this town—he was supposed to be famous."

How did I not know any of this? Then again, Jack and I never talk about either his life or Beth's. I don't know much about either one of them. "So what happened? He didn't make it to the NHL?"

Emmitt shakes his head. "Nah, he would've made it. He took a scholarship to Boston University. Your grandparents died in that car crash right after he went off to college, so he came back to take care of his little sister." He looks me right in the eye. "Your mom, I guess."

I stop skating and grab the wall for balance again, trying not to let it show how much that information floors me. My mom has always just told me her parents were dead. She's never mentioned that they died when she was so young, or that her brother basically raised her. I guess I shouldn't be too surprised, since she never even told me she had a brother. Still, it stings a little. Why didn't she ever tell us anything about her—our—family?

I manage to get my balance back, and we skate quietly for a few more moments before Emmitt looks at me, biting his lip. "Dusty, I've been wanting to talk to you. Do we mind if we give up skating and go sit in my truck or something?"

It's freezing outside, but I'm so curious to hear what Emmitt has to say that I'd probably sit in the arctic tundra with him.

"Sure."

We head outside in silence and keep up that silence while the truck warms up. I'm starting to wonder if this conversation is actually ever going to happen by the time he starts talking. "Dusty, I wanted to tell you that I'm really glad you came back. I was so mad when you left. Pissed at you for taking off without telling me, pissed at me for handling our whole thing the way I did." He starts rubbing his hands together, almost as if he's trying to keep them warm, despite the fact that's he's wearing thick mittens. "I mean, I really screwed that up."

Now he turns to face me, and I'm glad the truck is parked in a far-off corner of the parking lot where no one can see us, because anyone who can see his face right now would know for sure there's something between us. "I'm still not sure what I want, but you leaving… it showed me that I definitely want to be with you. I missed you, Dusty. I was really worried about you. I wanted to go to New York with Jack and find you, and then I wanted to come see you the second you got back. It really wrecked me that I couldn't *do* any of those things. It really wrecked me that I might be part of the reason you left."

I don't really want to tell him he's exactly right on that point, so I don't. "I want… I mean, I think you know what I want, Emmitt. But what about… everything else?"

The truck's pretty warm now, so he takes off his hat and runs his hands over his hair. "I still don't think I'm ready for the whole school to know or anything. I wish I was, I really do, Dusty. That's too much for me right now. But I'd like to hang out with you even more at school, and after school, and on the weekends. And...." He pulls off a mitten and raises a hand, places it against my cheek. "When it's just us, I'd like to be able to do whatever we want."

My heart's going a million miles an hour, and blood is pumping into areas of my body that really aren't appropriate to mention here, and all I want to do is lean in and make out with him. But if we're going to do this, I've got to be totally honest with him.

"I sort of told Jack. About me. About us. He was fine with it," I quickly blurt out.

Emmitt blushes, but he doesn't take his hand off my cheek. "I sort of told Casey too. He was way better about it than I thought he would be. I think... I think he's even happy for me. Or he will be."

That settled, he leans over, and I'm pretty sure he's about to kiss me. Because nobody else is around, and we can finally do whatever we want.

# CHAPTER
# NINE

*ONE AND a Half Years Earlier*

    *Dusty's dad hugged him hard and patted him on the back. "That should get you guys through for a while. It'll at least pay the rent. Tell your mom I said hi, okay?" His voice went stiff, and Dusty wondered when his parents had last actually talked to each other.*

    *"Sure, Dad." They were sitting on a bench in Acacia Park, looking at the mah-jongg court in front of them. "Uh, thanks for the money. Do you want to come back with me and see Matt and Julia? They miss you."*

    *His dad stood and stretched. "Nah, not today. Not while your mom's there. I'll stop by sometime after school while she's at work or something."*

    *Dusty had to stop himself from snorting. Lately his mother hadn't been spending too much time at work; Dusty had finally agreed to go beg their dad for money when he realized they were about to miss paying rent again.*

    *"Anyway, Dusty, Charlie and I got something to do this afternoon. I'll come by later this week, okay?" He hugged Dusty, and Dusty didn't even make the snide remark he wanted to make about not holding his breath. "That's my little Dusty-mop." Dusty half-groaned, half-smiled at his father's old nickname for him. His father had never liked the name Dustin very much—his mother had*

*chosen it—and he'd always called him either Dusty or that crazy nickname.*

*The house was quiet when he got back home. Matt and Julia were watching some cartoon on TV, and his mother was in the bathroom painstakingly doing her makeup. "Dusty! You're home, good. Did you see your dad?"*

*Dusty nodded and held up the cash he'd gotten at the park. "Excellent." His mother swooped into the room and grabbed it out of his hands. "I'll pay the rent. Then I'm going out with Sammy, so I need you to watch Matt and Julia, okay?"*

*Dusty groaned. He had a big test in a few days, and there were parent-teacher conferences coming up that she really needed to be there for. "Mom? With Sammy? You can't be gone too long this time. Conferences are on Friday, and if you aren't there, Mrs. Sabring will start asking me all kinds of weird questions again." Just like she had when their mom had missed the last conference.*

*"Dusty...." His mom trailed off. "Look, I just need some time away once in a while, okay? It's not easy being a single mom. This is hard for me." Her eyes welled up, and Dusty felt like screaming. He took a deep breath instead. If he yelled at her, she'd either start yelling back in front of Matt and Julia or disappear for who knew how long. "Once in a while is okay, mom. Even if you want to be gone all night tonight, that's okay. I can take care of them. But you really have to stop leaving for longer than that. Somebody's gonna notice soon."*

*Dusty's mom waved him off with a laugh. "Dusty, you worry far too much! Mothers leave their younger kids with their perfectly capable—" She leaned over to kiss Dusty's cheek. "—older children all the time. It will be fine, I promise."*

*She was out the door before Dusty could even finish saying good-bye.*

I FIND Jack in his study that night, grading papers. I've just read the kids a story and Beth has tucked them in. Ever since I came back,

Beth and I have started falling into a pattern of taking care of the kids together. It takes a lot of cooperation on both our parts, but it's working. Or at least, it seems to be.

"Hey, Jack?" I feel almost weird interrupting him. The study's really his space, just like Beth's office is hers. I don't really go into either one much.

"Hey Dusty." Jack smiles. "What's up?"

"Umm… are you busy? Can I talk to you a minute?"

"Of course we can talk." He puts down his pen and swirls his chair around to fully face me. "Drag up that old ottoman."

I don't know where to start. He stares at me easily, waiting. He's a teacher, I remember. He could probably wait for me all day.

"I… uh… I wanted to let you know that Emmitt and I talked today." Jack nods. "We're not going to tell anyone at school or anything, but I think he's sort of my boyfriend now." If feels strange saying that word out loud, labeling Emmitt like that. It's like the first time I said the word "gay" to Jack to describe myself: weird, but not wrong.

Jack's expression is unreadable. "I'm really glad you guys worked it out and all… but Dusty, are you going to be okay with keeping your relationship hidden? It's not going to be easy."

I know he's right, but I've thought about this. "Yeah, I really think I will. I mean, you and Casey know, and I'm going to tell Beth and Matt and Julia, so it will only be at school that we really keep it a secret. Plus, I'm new to this whole thing. I'm new to having a boyfriend, and I'm really new to being…." Somehow, I can't bring myself to say the word out loud again. "For now, at least, I think it will actually be easier for both of us this way."

Jack looks *really* happy now, and I wonder what the best way is to transition into a very different topic of conversation. I decide to go with blunt. "I was also wondering how my grandparents died."

Jack's face changes completely. . "I guess your mom never talked very much about them, huh?" I shake my head. "Well, they were great people, Dusty. Your grandmother was a homemaker and

138

your grandfather owned the farm this house used to go with. He gave it up when I was a kid and went to work for the post office—that's why the barn is gone—but he was always a farmer at heart. He kept a few chickens and whatnot in the shed. That's Beth's office now.

"I'd just left for college, and your mother was barely a freshman in high school, when he and your grandmother got into a car accident coming home from the store. Another car hit some ice and couldn't stop in time—a complete and utter accident."

"Oh," I say. It's like I'm being told the story of some far-off distant strangers, but these were my grandparents. In a lot of families, grandparents are a big part of kids' lives. Maybe they would have been part of mine too.

Jack turns back to his desk and pulls down a framed photo. "Those are your grandparents, Dusty."

They look… familiar. The picture is in black and white, but my grandfather seems to look just like Jack and I. So that's where it all started.

"Uh… Jack… did you take care of my mom after that?"

Jack bites his lip. "Yep, I did. I dropped out of BU to come back here, and I took part-time courses at UVM while she was still in school."

"Did you have to quit hockey?"

Jack sighs. "I suppose I didn't have to. But I was going to school part-time and working, and it was hard enough doing that and taking care of your mom at once. I decided taking care of my sister was more important than hockey, I guess." He stands and stretches. "We have more in common than you think, Dusty."

I stand too. "Wait, Jack, I don't get it… if you took care of my mom like that… why didn't you guys ever talk? Why didn't Mom tell us about you?"

Jack stands there, not answering, for a while. Finally he smiles. "Dusty… you know how close you are to Matt and Julia?"

139

"Well, yeah. I mean, that's why I have a hard time letting you and Beth take care of them, I guess."

"Well… with your mom and me, it was sort of the opposite situation. She hated and resented that I was taking care of her. She thought I was overbearing and suffocating, and she ran away from me the second she had her high school degree and enough money."

"My mom ran away?" This is kind of expected, actually. After all, she's been running away from the three of us for years. But it does make me think. I mean, what if Matt and Julia felt that way about me? What was so different between my mom and her kids that she couldn't enjoy having an older brother to watch out for her? "Were you?"

"Was I what?" Jack looks wholly confused by my question.

"Were you overbearing? Did you suffocate her?" I know it's a dangerous question, and I can tell from Jack's look that he's surprised I asked it, but somehow I have to know. Was it something I've done differently, or is it really that my Mom doesn't know how to do anything but run away?

Jack considers the questions carefully. "I guess…. I thought that all we had left was each other, and I acted that way. She saw the world a little differently…. She seemed to know she'd always have more than just me."

For the first time in my life, I feel like I understand my mother. But it isn't as good a feeling as I've always thought it would be.

Maybe I'm finally starting to understand Jack a little bit better too.

Jack keeps going. "At any rate, Abby ran away. I never heard from her again, and I didn't even know she'd had children until Ms. Davies called Beth and me. I loved your mother very much, Dusty. Very much. I can't tell you how happy I was to hear your middle name, to know there was some part of her that still loved me too."

We sit in that room for a while. Jack pulls out some old pictures of him and my mom as a child, and I tell him some stories from when Jules and Matt were younger, and even a few stories

140

from when I was younger. It feels good. There's one picture Jack shows me that I may hold forever in my head—my mom sitting by the back shed, long hair swinging in her face. She's laughing hard, holding onto a pair of ice skates, and Jack is hugging her, grinning. It sticks with me because she once took a picture of me and Matt, when he was really young, with Matt hugging me just like that, and I remember distinctly how much that picture made her smile. I tell Jack about that.

Finally it's late, and it seems like it's time to leave. "Oh," I say, halfway out the door, "you can call me Dustin. It's okay."

Jack raises an eyebrow. "Why? Why couldn't we call you that before?"

"Well... I dunno. It's just that Dad never called me anything but Dusty.... I sorta thought it should stay that way. Like Julia being Jules and all. But I think I'm ready for something different."

Jack nods. "I'll call you anything you want to be called, bud."

"GO, EMMITT, go!" Casey yells.

It's turning into a great afternoon. Casey and I are watching Emmitt work out with some of the other hockey players at the rink. They're getting ready for the season to start soon, and I'm already starting to realize that there isn't much I'd rather do than watch Emmitt skate around in a hockey uniform. I could do without watching him slam other guys into walls. Oh well. You can't have everything.

It's starting to feel like this thing between Emmitt and me is something real. I told Beth about Emmitt a few nights ago. She just hugged me and told me how happy she was for me; then she cried. I think she was so happy I was sharing something important with her that I probably could have told her I was dating a mutant and she would have been fine with it. I still haven't told Matt and Julia, mostly because I'm not sure how yet. Jack and Beth haven't pushed me to. They seem to think I'll figure it out on my own.

141

Icing on the cake to how well things are going? There's still no Rick around to hassle us. Word on Colby's one tiny street (that might be a little bit of an exaggeration) is that he's still in juvie. It's easier to keep enjoying his absence than worry about the day he shows back up at school.

Practice ends, and I try to not drool as I watch Emmitt tear off his helmet and skate over to the locker room. Casey just rolls his eyes. He has proven to be really good about us being together, but every now and then he likes to give us crap about it. "Dude, don't get your panties all in a twist," he says, poking me. "You get to hang out with him now, remember?" He pantomimes a kissy face, and I glare at him until he stops. We're still in public, after all, even if there aren't too many people around.

"Shuddup. Just because you can't get Rebecca Holstead to give you the time of day…."

He blushes and goes back to telling me, for the tenth time, why he just needs to get her to go out with him once and then he'll have her hooked.

Casey and I wait for Emmitt in the rink, and he drives us back to my house, where we're planning to watch movies, eat too much, and generally hang out. Casey has been complaining that Emmitt and I spend too much time without him now, so planning this evening was our way of getting him to shut up. We'll see if he's still so excited once he remembers that Matt has killer hero worship for Casey and will probably spend the entire night following him around everywhere he goes.

We pull up into the driveway and I zip up my jacket tightly around me in anticipation of the Vermont cold, which I am finally starting to get used to. We trudge through some snow piles. Casey is still going on about Rebecca. "Look, all I'm saying is that she doesn't know what I have to offer her yet…."

He's still talking, I think, but I've stopped listening, because I've just swung open the back door open and seen something I never thought I would see again. Sitting at the table, drinking a cup of coffee and holding Julia on her lap, is my mother.

Julia hops off of Mom's lap and comes running over to tug on my hand. "Dusty, Dusty! Mom's here! She's here and she likes my dogs!"

"Hello, Dusty." Mom is standing behind Jules now, smiling. "God, I've missed you." She reaches over for a hug and I immediately stiffen. Call it conditioning from years of being abandoned by this woman.

She turns to Emmitt and Casey and flashes them the sweet I-could-rob-a-bank-and-you'd-forgive-me-instantly-if-I-smiled smile that I know all too well. "Who are you?"

Emmitt, ever polite and respectful, pulls himself together the fastest. "Hello, Mrs. Porter. I'm Emmitt, and this is Casey. We're… friends with Dusty."

The door swings open behind us, and then Jack's home from the workout as well. He stops, stares an appropriate length of time, and then gathers his breath. "Abby. It's wonderful to see you."

"Jack! I've missed you so much!" She crosses the room and leans in for an enthusiastic hug, but when he hugs back, questions are written all over his face.

Jack glances over at me. I wonder what my face looks like right at that moment.

"Uh… Dustin, this might not be the best night for Emmitt and Casey to hang out with us. Boys, would you mind if we took a rain check?"

Emmitt nods; Casey is still frozen in place. Emmitt propels him toward the door. "I'll call you tomorrow," he calls over his shoulder, and he looks kind of anxious. Probably wondering if this means I'm going back to Colorado.

"Abby, it's been so long." Jack leaves his coat and hat in the mudroom, pulls off his boots, and walks into the kitchen to sit down across from Mom. Beth is sort of hiding by the sink, clutching at a cup of coffee. And I mean clutching—her knuckles are so white they look like they could burst open at any moment.

"I know, darling." She reaches over to squeeze his hand. "I really hadn't ever meant to be gone this long, but Colorado sort of became home. I got married, I had these three...." She gestures at Julia and me, and I realize I don't actually know where Matt is. "But I recently heard there was a mix-up when Julia got sick while Dusty was taking care of them. Is that true? Is that how they ended up here?"

A mix-up? Is she serious? She's *got* to be on drugs about as hard-core as whatever my Dad's on. I'm just about to pipe in with something when Jack interrupts me. "Dustin? Will you take Julia upstairs?"

"Dustin? What happened to Dusty?" Mom looks over at me, puzzled.

I ignore her and grab Jules's hand. "Sure, Jack."

I start leading Julia upstairs and stop next to Beth. "Where's Matt?" I whisper to her.

Beth seems surprised to find me standing in front of her. "Oh... he ran up to his room when your mom got here. I went to go talk to him, but he said he wanted to be alone." This is disconcerting. I nod at Beth, hoping she'll know what that means better than I do, and I take off up the stairs with Julia struggling to keep up.

Matt is face-down on his bed when we get there. I grab his shoulder. "Matt, are you okay? What's wrong?"

When he finally looks up at me, his face is bright red. He's obviously been crying. "What do you think? Mom's back!"

I've already figured that out, but I'm still not sure why Matt is crying. He's always been pretty excited to see Mom before.

Matt flips over on his back. "She's going to take us away, Dusty! Back to Colorado! And I won't get to play soccer anymore, and you'll have to go back to cooking dinner and cleaning, we'll never see Aunt Beth and Uncle Jack again, just like we never did before."

I could feel a frown slipping across my face. "Did you hate it there, Matt? With just the three of us? Was it that bad?"

Matt reads my mind instantly. "Dusty, I didn't mean that! I liked living with you! But I like it here too, and here I get to play soccer!"

That makes me smile. It's true. We *never* had money for Matt to play soccer in Colorado.

"I *hate* her!" he pronounces fervently. "She can't just come and go when she wants! Parents have to stay with their kids!" He says it with such gusto that I don't really know how to respond.

Julia pulls on my shirtsleeve. "Dusty? I love Mom, but I love Beth too. Can we stay with them both?"

No use lying now, I figure. "Julia... probably not."

"Oh." She frowns, and her face crinkles up before she starts to cry. "Matt's right. I don't wanna go home! And I don't want Mom to leave again!"

Great. Five minutes into this conversation and I've got one of them in tears and the other on the brink.

By the time I finally get Matt and Julia calmed down and convince Matt to read Julia a story, I've decided I'd like to know more about what Mom's plans are.

Beth is sitting alone at the kitchen table, still clutching that coffee mug. I can hear Mom and Jack talking in the study, but all I can make out are strange, toneless whispers.

"Hi, Beth."

She looks up at me. "They're in the study, Dustin... if you want to talk to them."

"Yeah, I will. Uh, Beth... just so you know... Matt's pretty upset about Mom coming back... and then Jules was too.... Maybe you could go upstairs and read with them?"

Beth's eyes sag with happiness. "Thank you, Dustin," she whispers. "You have no idea how much that means to me."

Actually, I'm pretty sure I do.

I head to the study door. I barely have my hand on the door handle when the voices inside suddenly become loud enough for me to make out exactly what everyone is saying.

145

"Jack, I know I haven't been the best mother in the world, but I don't see what you're so upset about. I don't see what anyone is so upset about. For crying out loud, I wouldn't have left them alone if I didn't think Dusty could handle it!"

"Abby, he's fourteen! You don't leave a fourteen-year-old alone with little kids! What if he hadn't known enough to take Julia to the hospital when she had appendicitis? What would have happened?"

"Jack, you always think like that! You can never just look on the bright side! That didn't happen, all right? Julia's fine! She's fine, and she wants to see me!"

"Yeah, because she hasn't seen you in months! It's amazing she remembers who you are!"

"I can't believe you would say something like that! You know how much I love my kids!"

"No, Abby, I don't! In fact, I have very little idea, because up until a few months ago, I didn't know they existed!"

I open the door and they both stop, mouths still open, eyes still wide with anger. "Dusty!" Mom exclaims.

"Hey." I shove my hands in my pockets.

"Dusty," Mom says again, coming over to cup my face in her hands. "God, you've grown." She pats my cheek. "Jack, I'd like a moment alone with Dusty, please."

Jack seems to consider for a moment whether or not he should do that. Finally he crosses the room, resting his hand lightly on my shoulder for a moment before he leaves.

"So," Mom says, gesturing widely for me to sit on the ottoman while she flops into Jack's desk chair, "what's been going on?" She smiles brightly, as if I'm about to tell her about a trip I just took to Fiji.

"Well… uh… Julia got appendicitis, and they found out it was just the three of us living in the apartment, so we came out here, and, uh, it's been okay here."

"Jack mentioned you tried to run away not long ago."

"Yeah, I guess I did. But it's fine now. The kids really like it here," I add.

Mom waves that comment off with her hand. "Oh, they're good kids, they like anything." Her hair, exactly like Julia's, is very long now—all the way down her back. When Julia was little, she used to love playing with it. "Dusty, I know you haven't always been happy with how I've taken care of you." She stands and suddenly starts pacing around the small office. "It was a rather huge shock for me to find out that you and Matt and Julia had been taken away without me even knowing about it. An enormous shock. It really opened up my eyes to a lot of things." She's starting to tear up, but I'm used to Mom crying when she wants to get her way, so it doesn't affect me much anymore. "I want to try again, Dusty. I want to be a better mother this time, I really do. I came all the way here to convince Jack—and you—that I can do better. I'll start working full-time again, and I'll make sure not to stay out all night anymore, and I'll be there for you guys. Really, Dusty, I will this time." She sits down again, and now the tears are flowing freely. "I know it's hard for you to believe. If I were you, I wouldn't believe me either. But Dusty, I really have learned now. I've finally learned what you were trying to tell me."

I'm like a deer in the headlights or something. I mean, come on. What am I supposed to say to that? May as well let her know what she's up against, I figure. "Mom... uh... you should know that Matt's pretty upset with you. He likes it here, and I don't know if he'll want to leave."

Mom sighs. "I suppose I deserve that. I'll speak to him tomorrow." She yawns. "I'm exhausted. Think I'll hit the sack. Who sleeps in my old room these days?"

"Me." She should like that, I think.

Mom leans over to kiss me. "Bunk with your brother tonight, okay?" she says. "I used to love that room; I've missed it. And listen, Dusty.... I'm going to hang around a while, convince Jack that I love you guys, and then we'll go home, I promise. And I'll finally be the mom you've probably wanted all these years."

147

She floats out of the room. My mother has never walked anywhere—she always manages to float somehow.

THE FIRST time both my parents disappeared at once, leaving me alone with the kids, I floundered, trying to figure out how to feed them and get them to school and daycare. I was nervous and edgy all the time, but I was determined not to let anyone know what was going on. I felt a constant sense of agitation or unease, as if everything I knew could unravel at any moment—only I wasn't entirely certain I didn't want it to.

That is exactly how I feel now. I don't know what to say to Matt and Julia anymore. Julia keeps asking me questions—are we going with Mom? Can she keep her dogs? Matt is distant and angry, avoiding everyone in the house. I'm totally aware that there's a huge power struggle unfolding before my eyes and not really sure whose side I'm supposed to be on—but even that's getting clearer and clearer.

At breakfast the next morning, as Beth is feeding the kids and I'm trying unsuccessfully to figure out the biology homework I never figured out the night before, Mom comes swooping into the kitchen in a large blue bathrobe. "Morning, loves!" She kisses each of us on the head one at a time, totally oblivious to the fact that Matt ducks out of the way. "Oh, I'm so excited to bring you to school again. It's been so long!" She pours a cup of coffee for herself and leans against the counter.

"Morning, everyone." Jack comes into the kitchen, stopping for a second to tie his shoes. He kisses Beth and Jules and pats Matt on the head, but he and Mom never lock eyes. "Dustin, can you be ready to go in five?"

I give up on biology and move the kids toward the front hallway to help them get their shoes on before I leave. It's a routine Beth and I have developed, and Matt and Julia are very used to it, but Mom puts her coffee mug down and comes swooping over.

"Dusty, let me help them. Oh, and Beth, would you mind if I took them to school this morning? If I borrowed your car?"

Beth blinks a few times before she answers. "Well… Abby… why don't we just take them together? Go get dressed; school starts soon."

Jack and I don't move. I'm standing with one hand on each of the kids' shoulders; he's standing with his arm around Beth. Mom is alone, in the center of the room, not even the coffee mug attached to her at that moment.

Mom laughs, and the sound fills the room suddenly and awkwardly. "Of course I'll get dressed, but let's take our time—no need to rush. Maybe they could even stay home this morning. They could miss half a day of school to see their mother!" She looks eagerly at both of them, and Julia walks right into it.

"Yeah! Yeah! Let's stay home!"

Matt crosses his arms. "No. I have a test this morning. Aunt Beth, can we leave?"

Jack glances at Beth and comes over to where I am standing. "Abby, the kids can't miss school right now. Listen, tonight we'll all go out together, to dinner or something. Dustin and I need to leave, and Beth needs to get to work."

The look Mom gives Jack became harder and harder as he speaks. Then she suddenly shrugs and smiles. "Of course, there's plenty of time. I'll just get dressed and go with Beth to drop them off." She swoops out of the room again, kissing me as she goes.

On the way to school, Jack and I don't say much. Finally, Jack asks what I've been asking myself all morning. "So, do you want to go back to Colorado with your mom?"

"No." The answer leaves my mouth before I even have time to think about it, and for the first time in a long time, I feel like I know exactly what I want. "Oh. No. I did, I mean, I thought I did. I guess I don't anymore. I guess… I kind of like it here now. I'd miss a lot of stuff." Like Emmitt. And Casey. And skateboarding and hockey and Jack's cooking and even Jack. I just can't make myself say that out loud yet.

Jack doesn't smile or frown or change his facial expression at all. It's pretty clear he'd thought I'd say that all along. "Dustin, this could get rough. Your mother seems convinced she can regain custody of the three of you, and I don't think the courts are going to give her that. I'm really not sure how this whole thing is going to turn out."

"It's not going to be a problem." I say it steadily.

"What do you mean it isn't going to be a problem?" Jack's definitely shocked that I'm brushing the whole thing off.

"Jack…." I stare out the window. "What did Mom do when she didn't like living with you anymore? What does Mom do when she gets sick of taking care of us? What does Mom do… well, whenever anything gets hard?"

Neither of us answers that question, because it doesn't seem necessary.

Jack races us both out of school that afternoon. He even gets annoyed when I take a few minutes trying to borrow Casey's French notes. I know he's worried about leaving my mom alone with Beth and the kids.

I'm not in much hurry to stay, anyway. School's been about as awkward as it can be. Both Emmitt and Casey have asked me what's going on with my mom, and I just shrugged and told them I wasn't sure. It's pretty clear they want to know more. Emmitt, especially, has been practically biting back questions every time we met up at my locker.

Part of me wants to assure him I'm not going anywhere, but I don't really want to talk about the whole thing right now. This is one of those days when our whole "secret relationship" is actually working in my favor. There's no way he can try to dig too deep without everyone noticing there's something going on between the two of us.

Jack and I get back to the house, and everything is surprisingly calm. Matt and Julia are working quietly at the kitchen table doing their homework, Mom sitting beside them and putting in helpful hints every now and then. Matt is still glaring at her intermittently, but she doesn't seem to notice. Beth is puttering around the kitchen, cleaning up. Mom smiles when she sees us come in and motions me over for a hug.

So far, so good. Thing is? I am 1000 percent positive this is the calm before the storm.

Jack takes us all out to the Chinese Buffet in Colby for dinner, which is this small hole-in-the-wall restaurant with really great food. I'm only on my second plate when Mom starts in.

"Matthew," she says, "I was thinking that once we get back to Colorado Springs, we could finally get that dog you've been asking for."

"I already have a dog," he says coolly, taking a bite of lo mein. "Right here. And I don't want to go back to Colorado Springs."

"Honey...." She smiles at him and starts stroking his hair. "I know you're mad at me, and I don't blame you. But I promise you, I'm different now. Things at home will be different. I'll stay home with you, and we'll get a dog. It will be wonderful!"

"Things are wonderful *now*." Matt goes back to his lo mein again, still calm, but there's an edge to his voice.

"Matt, I promise that if you just give me a chance...."

Suddenly Matt is out of his seat and shouting. "You never keep your promises! You promised you'd come with me on field trips and take us to the park and make us special dinners and then you'd just go away and it would never happen!"

"What, honey?" Her eyes are wide, lost, as though she has no idea who is speaking to her. Maybe she doesn't.

"Uncle Jack's a great uncle! He plays with us and he makes dinner for us and Aunt Beth is great too! Way better than you! I hate you! I wish you'd go away and never come back!" He ends with a great flourish, throwing his fork down on the ground and running out the door.

"Matt!" I holler loudly as I throw down my own fork to chase after him.

Matt's nowhere to be seen outside. The buffet is in the middle of a small shopping plaza with about five stores in it, but it's on the edge of the downtown area, and Matt could have gone anywhere. Jack comes racing up behind me, with Beth, Mom, and Jules behind him.

Jack plants his hand firmly on my shoulder. "Beth and I will go looking for him. You stay here with your mom and Julia."

"Jack!" I don't say anything else; I don't need to.

He rolls his eyes. "Fine. Beth and Abby, you stay here with Julia in case he comes back." I get that he doesn't want to leave my mom alone with Julia, and I don't really blame him. "We'll find him," he adds reassuringly to Beth.

Jack takes off in one direction and I take off in the other, completely terrified. What if Matt runs out in front of a car? What if we never find him? What if I never see him again? I think about that a little too long and realize this is probably how Matt felt when I'd tried to run away to Colorado.

I'm circling the street in front of an optometrists' office when I realize I need to think like Matt. If I were Matt, where would I run to?

It only takes a second before I pull out my cell phone and call Jack. "Sports store!" I yell loudly. "Check the sports store!" I hang up and start running down the street.

I see him running up toward the sports store from the other direction just as I get there. We look at each other, say nothing, and go inside in together.

We find Matt sitting in the back of the soccer section, between the balls and the shin pads. He's wadded up in a ball on the floor, crying.

Derek, the guy who owns the store and also knows Jack pretty well, comes up to us and puts his hand on Jack's shoulder. "Hey, man. I tried calling your house, but no one answered your phone. I was just calling around to get your cell phone number."

Jack nods. "Thanks." We both lean down on either side of Matt and slowly unroll him from his ball.

He's still crying, holding his hands over his face, apparently embarrassed to be caught like that. "I hate her…. I hate her…. I hate her…." he keeps saying over and over again.

I pull Matt into a sitting position, and we sit on either side of him.

"You know what, Matt?" Jack sighs. "Dustin and I don't blame you at all. But you have to remember, she's a person just like all of us. And people make mistakes, Matt."

Matt pokes his head out of my lap and looks at us. "I used to hate her all the time," I tell him quietly. "Even when I went... away... to look for her, it wasn't because I really wanted to find her or anything." I don't bother to try to explain that to Matt. He probably understands, anyway. I'm starting to think Matt understands a lot more than I've been giving him credit for. "But I don't really want to hate her anymore, Matt. It takes a lot of energy to hate someone, and I don't want to use my energy that way anymore. I don't think you should, either."

Matt looks at me, wide-eyed. "Why does she keep saying she wants to take us back there, Dusty? I don't want to go back."

I frown, because I don't really know the answer to that. "You know, Matt... even though Mom was pretty bad at taking care of us, I think she always wanted to try. She always came home, right? That's more than we can say for Dad. I think this is just her trying again."

Matt snuggles into me. "She should stop trying, I think," he sniffles. "She's just not good at being a mom. Beth is way better."

Jack smiles at him. "Well, Matt," he says, "Beth's not going anywhere."

Matt nods, suddenly very grave-looking. He stands up and wipes his face on his sleeve. "I'm ready to go home now," he says seriously.


I WAKE up in the middle of the night to creaks on the stairs. I know those creaks. They're the creaks the stairs to the attic bedroom make.

She's leaving again already. Part of me wants to let her disappear into the night. The ride home from Colby was torturous,

Matt never looking at Mom and Julia filling the silence by telling us about some artwork of hers. I wondered all the way home if Mom could even last the night. Now I know she can't.

But I can't just let her leave. I can't let her get away with that again. So I start down the stairs after her.

"Going somewhere?" I catch her in the kitchen, getting together a bag and putting on shoes.

She looks up, not at all surprised to find me in the doorway. "Yes. You three seem happy here. I see now that you don't need me anymore."

"That's not fair, Mom. That's completely unfair. You made us not need you." My voice is angry and desperate. I *am* desperate. Desperate for her to understand that this isn't something we've done on purpose. "You left us alone all the time. We had to *learn* not to need you."

Mom's eyes are welling up with tears, but I keep talking. "I didn't like it, Mom, but we had no choice. Dad took off and then you were always taking off too."

"Dusty… I…." Mom stops and sighs.

She picks up her bags and walks into the front hallway. "Just tell the kids I love them, okay? Tell them that once in a while. I love you."

And then she's gone. The door slams behind her, and I hear a car roar up the driveway. She must have called a cab; how long has she been planning to leave?

I turn to go back upstairs, and I find Jack standing in the kitchen in his sweats—it's pretty obvious he's been standing there for awhile, but he never made a sound. "Hey, kiddo." Jack flips on the overhead lamps. "I think I'm going to make some hot chocolate. You want some?"

I just nod and sink into a chair. Jack puts some water on to boil before he comes over and sits down beside me. "Dustin…."

I roll my eyes. "I know, I know, the 'I know this hasn't been easy for you' speech. Yeah, it really hasn't. But the kids like it here, and I'm beginning to like it here, and Mom... well, Mom'll just always be Mom and Dad'll always be Dad."

Jack looks at me innocently. "Oh. I was just going to say that we didn't have any marshmallows."

I just roll my eyes again.

"Hey, Dustin?" he finally asks after a few minutes.

"What, we outta cookies too?"

He smirks. "Actually, we are. But that isn't what I was going to say. I was going to say...." He hesitates. "You know, Rick's time in juvie will be up eventually, and he'll be coming back to school."

"You're just a ray of sunshine tonight, Jack."

He grins. "Maybe a strange time to bring that up. But I was thinking a lot over the past few days about how much more you seem to trust me now, Dustin. That matters to me. I want to make sure that's something we can keep going even after Rick's in school again. Do you know what I'm saying?"

I blink a few times, studying him carefully.

It's crazy how fast things can change, isn't it?

"Yeah, Jack," I finally say. "I know what you're saying."

We're both silent for a while before I realize I have something I need to ask.

"Hey, Jack? Do you think it'd be okay if I call my friend Race sometime? You know, from the Springs?"

Jack stands and stretches, then walks over to the stove to pour out boiling water into mugs. "Absolutely, Dustin. Call him anytime you want."

I stare out the window. It's started snowing a little bit, and tiny flakes are floating by the window. "So, you coming to our next hockey workout?" Jack asks, adding hot chocolate mix to the mugs.

"Yeah. Of course. Emmitt would kill me if I missed it."

Jack snorts. "Well, at least he's making sure you become a proper hockey fan, just as all Vermonters should be."

"Whatever. I mean, you're the one who's going to have to deal with my report card when I get a D in history because I was too busy trying to figure out that stupid sport to do the research for my history project."

"Right. What's this project on? And when is it due? I need to know how to hold your nose to the grindstone."

"Zeb Pike. You know, the guy who didn't make it to the top of Pikes Peak but still got the mountain named after him. He got stuck in the snow, you know."

Jack starts laughing into his hot cocoa. "Actually, I never knew that. He really got stuck in the snow? Climbing the mountain they named after him?"

I toss a napkin at him. "Look, Jack, just because you have no appreciation for knowing when to give up on something…." I suddenly remember things both Mr. Lewis and Jed have said to me. "I wanna find out more about how he knew he needed to go back down."

Jack shrugs and looks out the window at the tire tracks Mom's cab left, which are already disappearing under the falling snow. "You're right, Dusty. That is something to learn more about."

# EPILOGUE

"DUSTIN, CAN you get a start on setting the table? They'll be here soon."

Beth's calling from the kitchen again, and her voice sounds mildly panicked. I'm not sure what she's so worried about. It's not her boyfriend's family that's coming over for Thanksgiving dinner today.

It *was* her idea to invite Emmitt and Casey and their mother over for dinner, and I was actually pretty excited when she suggested it.

Then Emmitt got the bright idea to tell his mother about us after Thanksgiving dinner, and ever since then my stomach hasn't stopped churning.

I head into the kitchen, which smells really good, and start gathering the stuff to set the dining room table. I'm nearly done when the phone rings, and Jack comes into the room to tell me it's for me.

"Hello?" I'm holding the cordless phone with my shoulder and juggling a whole stack of silverware and placemats, so it's impressive I don't drop them all when I hear a voice say, "Hey. It's Race."

157

I put down the pile of stuff in my hands and sit down. I called him almost a week ago and hadn't heard back from him yet, so I was pretty sure we were never going to talk again. "Oh. Race. Happy Thanksgiving."

"Um, yeah. Happy Thanksgiving."

Silence.

"Listen, Dusty, I really am sorry about everything that went down. It was just hard to watch how rough things were for you sometimes, and that day when you heard about Vermont, I was thinking that maybe you'd finally get to be happy. I didn't mean to make it sound like I didn't want you to leave or something. I really miss you, dude. It's not the same without you here."

I've always known that, but it still feels good to hear him say it out loud. "Race… you don't have to say you're sorry. You were the only person who ever helped me… well, you know when. I owe you, man. I shouldn't have yelled at you that day." I pause. "Plus, you ended up being right. It turned out kind of okay here. I am happier."

"Yeah? You like it there?"

"Yeah. My aunt and uncle are okay, and I'm skateboarding a lot, or I was until it got balls cold, and Matt and Julia are really happy. You were pretty much right. It was a good thing."

We start talking about school and the Springs. He gets me caught up on what's going on with our group of friends. Daniel got suspended for putting a stink bomb in the boys' bathroom. I'm not really surprised. Race is failing English. Ms. Carlson, he says, is still droning on. "Jenni flat-out fell asleep in her class the other day—drooling and everything, dude—and she didn't even notice."

That makes me laugh. "Ms. Carlson. That woman got me all into studying Zebulon Pike. I'm doing a huge history report on him."

"On Zeb Pike? The guy who didn't even finish climbing Pikes Peak and got arrested later on? Really? He always seemed like kind of a loser to me."

"Yeah, I kind of thought maybe he was too, at first. Then I started doing all this research on him, about why he didn't finish climbing the mountain and how it got its name and all that, and you know what? It turns out he actually did a lot of stuff. He was one of the first guys to map that part of Colorado, and he discovered a bunch of other things there, and everywhere he went, he wrote what he saw down in these journals. People all over the world read them. That stuff is really why he got a mountain named after him. And the arrest and stuff... well, a lot of rough stuff happened to him. But exploring new territory isn't probably going to be easy, you know?"

"Huh." Race is silent for a minute. "Did it make you miss Colorado? Doing all that research?" He sounds a little hesitant.

I don't have to think very hard to answer that question. "I mean, I'll always miss Colorado." I take a deep breath. "But I can go back. I'll be like Zeb, you know? See what's out there. I'll come back there. You know I will." This is all getting too philosophical for me, so I change the subject and start telling him how Julia and Matt are doing.

After we hang up, I realize I didn't tell him about Emmitt.

I guess that will have to be a mountain for another day.

JOHANNA PARKHURST grew up on a small dairy farm in northern Vermont before relocating to the rocky mountains of Colorado. She spends her days helping teenagers learn to read and write and her evenings writing things she hopes they'll like to read. She strives to share stories of young adults who are as determined, passionate, and complex as the ones she shares classrooms with.

Johanna holds degrees from Albertus Magnus College and Teachers College, Columbia University. She loves traveling, hiking, skiing, watching football, and spending time with her incredibly supportive husband. You can contact her at johannawriteson@gmail.com or find her on Twitter at https://twitter.com/johannawriteson.

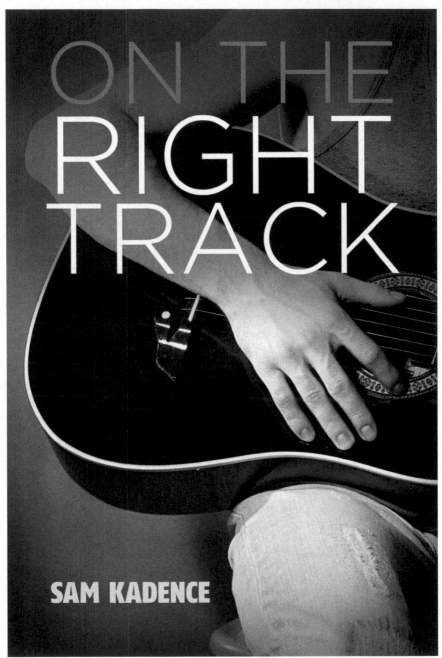

OMORPHI

lucabni

C. KENNEDY

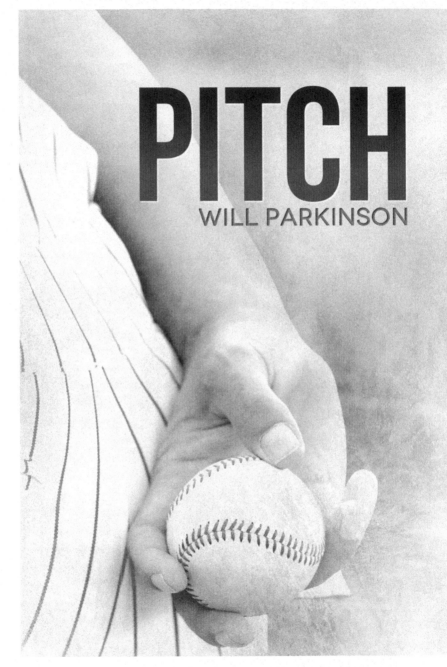

PITCH

WILL PARKINSON

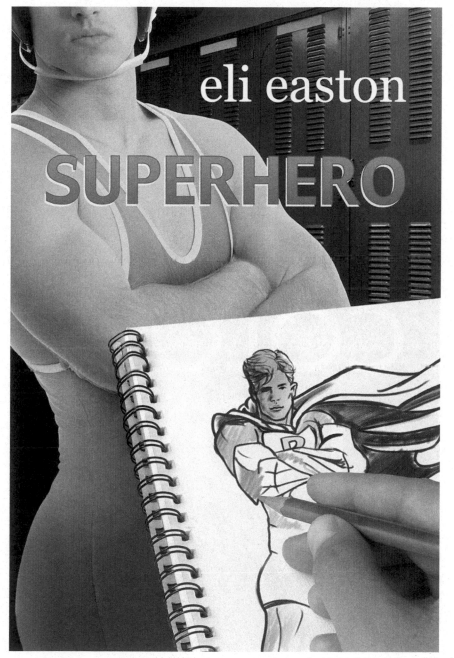

eli easton

SUPERHERO

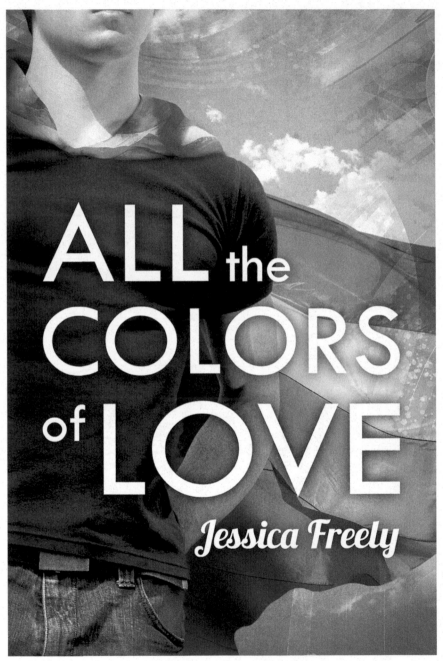

ALL the
COLORS
of LOVE

*Jessica Freely*

Also from HARMONY INK PRESS

J.R. LENK

Collide

http://www.harmonyinkpress.com

Harmony Ink

CPSIA information can be obtained
at www.ICGtesting.com
Printed in the USA
LVOW01s0117020217
522883LV00024B/1239/P